JOHNNY

the

Amazing

PARROT

& Friends

Rich &
Mikie Web

iUniverse, Inc.
New York   Bloomington

Johnny the Amazing Parrot & Friends

Copyright © 2010 by Rich and Mikie Web

iUniverse books may be ordered through booksellers or by contacting:
iUniverse
1663 Liberty Drive
Bloomington, IN 47403
www.iuniverse.com
1-800-Authors (1-800-288-4677)

Because of the dynamic nature of the Internet, any Web addresses or links contained in this book may have changed since publication and may no longer be valid. This is a work of fiction. All of the characters, names, incidents, organizations, and dialogue in this novel are either the products of the author's imagination or are used fictitiously.

ISBN: 978-1-4502-3596-9 (pbk)
ISBN: 978-1-4502-3597-6 (ebk)

Printed in the United States of America
iUniverse rev. date: 9/9/10

Johnny was brought to the United States, from the jungles of Africa. He was sold to a local pet store in Roseville, Virginia, where he was given the name of Johnny. He is a fifteen-inch Yellow—Headed Amazon Oratrix and, appears to be about four years old. Later, a man named Howard Udall, (known as Hud) purchased him. Hud is an ex-Navy Seal member, and is a forty-five year old bachelor, who works for NCIS as an investigator. His apartment is in Roseville, Virginia; a quiet little town located forty miles south of Washington, DC.

Hud became acquainted with Johnny, when he stopped into the pet store to buy food for his many species of fish he has in his aquarium. Hud was thinking about stopping for pizza and beer on his way home. As he is walking past the parrot cages he hears a voice saying, "pizza and beer sure sounds good to me too." Hud looks up at the parrot and thinks, what's up with this crazy bird. Johnny looks up; "I'm not crazy, just hungry and thirsty."

Hud asks Johnny, "how did you know what I was thinking?" "I can read minds, but please don't tell anyone, especially the storekeeper. I don't trust him, he always has bad thoughts." Hud asks, "read my mind again, what am I thinking?" "You are thinking about buying me." Hud asks him a few more questions and realizes this parrot can read minds. For the parrot's own safety I need to get him out of here.

Hud walks up to the check out counter, and pays the storekeeper for Johnny. The clerk takes Johnny out of his cage and he flies onto Hud's shoulder. The two of them leave the pet shop with Johnny squawking, "let's blow this pop stand." On the way home they stop for pizza and beer and have a long conversation about Johnny's life.

A sharp whistle followed by a shrill "Wow! Pretty girls!" penetrate the foyer of the local shopping center. "It's a parrot!" a young girl exclaims as she sees Johnny perched on the shoulder of his owner. He cuts quite a figure with his brightly colored tail feathers gently cascading down the back of Hud's leather jacket. Hud continues through the mall, as Johnny, sitting proudly on his shoulder, maintains a careful eye out for more pretty girls, or whatever adventure might be just around the corner.

Johnny loves adventure! None of this normal parrot stuff for him! If it isn't a new adventure forget it! Johnny scans the crowd, his mind open to any intriguing thoughts that some unsuspecting shopper might be harboring. You see Johnny is a very special parrot. He has many amazing talents not the least of which, is his ability to read minds. While reading the minds of unsuspecting people is entertainment for Johnny, it sometimes gets him into trouble. It also has, more than once, proven to be a blessing.

The two of them enter a department store to look for new socks for Hud. As a bachelor, when Hud does his laundry at the Laundromat his socks somehow disappear. When he was putting his socks away he noticed he is down to about twenty miss-matched socks. Johnny raises his head, "oh, oh, bad man! bad man!" he whispers in Hud's ear as Hud ruffles through the many pairs of socks on the counter, trying to decide just which one might be appropriate for his next trip out of town. As a covert agent for the NCIS, Hud quite often, is required to be out of the country, and must always be prepared to leave on a moment's notice.

Finally getting Hud's attention, Johnny motions to the right with his head, "I'm reading that guy's mind and he's planning to grab the girl walking just ahead of him." Hud trying to appear nonchalant, while spotting the girl and the suspicious man. He quickly pays for his selected socks. He and Johnny leave the Mall just behind the young girl. The suspected kidnaper elbows his way through the crowd to get in place behind her. With Johnny and Hud following closely, the girl, and the suspect each get into their own cars. Hud quickly takes note of the license number, as he and Johnny quickly get into Hud's car. As the girl pulls out of the parking lot, Hud manages to get between her car and the suspect's car. In the heavy traffic, the suspect is forced to lose sight of the young girl.

"Once again, you've proven what a special parrot you really are," Hud remarks as he gently rubs Johnny's head. "I'll enter all the information of the man on my computer, as soon as we get home. Once that is done, I'll alert my police buddy Bill." Johnny knows, Hud's police buddy is Lt. Bill Boyd, and draws a sigh of relief knowing that Bill will get involved, and get this scum-bag off the streets.

Johnny rolls his eyes as the phone rings. From the urgency in Hud's voice, Johnny suspects the caller is Hud's boss, Gary Bertram. Following a short conversation, Hud explains to Johnny, "Gary needs me as soon as possible in Iraq. It seems two high officials are suspected of stealing large sums of money and selling guns to Al-Qaida. Gary needs someone he can trust to investigate the situation right away. I'll ask Mrs. Handly to watch you while I'm gone."

Greta Handly, Hud's elderly landlady, lives downstairs from Hud and Johnny's apartment. Johnny isn't too excited about spending time with her, and she doesn't like it when Johnny talks or sings too loud. She is a stout woman known to get into the sauce and can really get ornery when she's drinking. She and Johnny do have one thing in common, Johnny loves beer too. Mrs. Handly, however, doesn't like to share her beer. Hud only allows Johnny to have a few sips, and when Johnny drinks too much, he breaks into song with, "One hundred bottles of beer on the wall." Not a bad voice, just very loud!

Hud knocks loudly on Mrs. Handly's door, as he knows she is hard of hearing. After several loud knocks, Mrs. Handly appears. "Can Johnny stay with you again

until I come back from Iraq? I'll give you a hundred dollars
a week this time." Johnny thinks, maybe she won't let me
stay. No such luck, that offer of a hundred dollars a week
did the trick. "Of course, I'd love to have his company."
She lied. Her mind is saying something different; Johnny
muses as he taps into her mind. Mrs. Handly smiles at
Hud, but she is thinking, the money will sure come in
handy, but this is the last time I am watching that noisy
old bird. He really gets on my nerves, and he'd better stay
out of my beer too.

Hud and Johnny go back upstairs to get Johnny's
favorite toys. "Come on, Johnny, let's go, Mrs. Handly
is waiting for us." Johnny reluctantly follows down the
stairs to Mrs. Handly's apartment. "I'll be back as soon
as I can." Hud explained. He gently rubs Johnny's head.
"Be a good boy." Johnny's eyes follow Hud to the door.
"Johnny be good boy!" he squawked.

As night falls, Mrs. Handly finishes her glass of beer
and passes out at the table. Johnny, already missing his
pal, thinks maybe, some of that beer will help him sleep.
Quietly slipping past Mrs. Handly, Johnny approaches
the refrigerator. It's hard work to get that refrigerator
door open, but Johnny thinks it's worth the trouble if he
can get some beer. Grabbing a towel, he slips it through
the handle on the door of the refrigerator. Then grasping
the ends of the towel with his teeth, he gives a yank—
nothing happens. "Oh, well, if at first you don't succeed,
try, try, again." Grasping the ends of the towel again with

his teeth, Johnny gives one last pull. Sha-sam, it opens! "Now, where's the beer? I see it - right there." Johnny spreads his wings and skooches around until he can reach the beer with his wing. One good push with his strong wing, and the beer moves forward. He then reaches both wings in and grabs the can of beer. Along side of the beer, Johnny spies a slice of leftover pizza. Perfect with the beer he thinks as he pulls the pizza out of the refrigerator. "A straw would be nice," Johnny said, as he looks around the kitchen. "There they are." He pulls the tab of the can with his teeth, and inserts the straw, and sucks down half the beer. Grabbing a bite of the pizza, "aah life is good, he sighed. I don't mind staying here at all, as long as the old lady sleeps." Upon finishing the beer and pizza, he stumbles over to the couch and soon, he too is sleeping.

Upon awakening, Mrs. Handly gets up and staggers to the refrigerator looking for that last can of beer. The beer is gone! "What the . . . where's my beer?" As she looks around the kitchen, her eyes land on Johnny sleeping comfortably on the couch.

"So it was you!" She yelled. Johnny shakes his head as he tries to wake up. He can't figure out what's going on. Mrs,, Handly rushes toward him, swinging her broom. One swipe, after another barely misses Johnny, but one mighty blow finds Johnny on the floor. "This is the last straw you dumb noisy bird!" With that, she sweeps Johnny across the floor and out the door. She then slams the door, "good riddance!" she yelled.

Johnny tries to stand up but discovers his leg won't support him. Mrs. Handly and her broom had done a good job. Johnny lies on the ground wondering what in the world he can do now. If only Hud was here, he thought. He's been gone for only a few hours and already I'm in trouble! Maybe I can just lay here until he gets home. Johnny's thoughts are interrupted when he hears footsteps. As they come into sight, Johnny recognizes the two kids he has seen playing outside his apartment window. Jimmy and Amie Winters, the twins, live just a block away. As they come closer, Johnny says over and over, "Johnny's hurt—Johnny's hurt." Suddenly, Amie shrieks, "Oh my gosh, look at the parrot it looks hurt." Jimmy reaches down and gently picks Johnny up. "I just got the crap beat out of me," Johnny moaned. "Who did this to you?" Jimmy asked. "That ornery old landlady, Mrs. Handly. She hates me. Just wait til Hud comes home. He'll show her. Can you kids take care of me until he gets home? I just need a warm place to stay. I don't eat much, and I would never ever touch your daddy's beer!" "You really talk good," Amie says. "What's your name?" Johnny asked." My name is Amie, and this is my twin brother Jimmy." Glad to make your acquaintance. My name is Johnny. Thank you for finding me I thought I was going to die here."

Amie runs and knocks on Mrs. Handly's door. Mrs. Handly answers the door. "Is this your parrot?" Amie asked. "Nope, it ain't my bird. He belongs to the man who lives upstairs." "Why did you hurt him?" Amie demanded. "That ain't none of your business, and you'd better get him out of here before I finish him off. He's a pain in the neck. Here's a pen and paper. Give me your name and phone number, and when his owner calls, I'll have him contact you."

"C'mon Johnny, we'll take you home with us. Mrs. Bellinger will know what to do, and you are going to be just fine." Mrs. Bellinger lives with the Winters family. She is their live-in housekeeper but more like a grandmother to Jimmy and Amie. She has lived with them since the separation of their parents.

Mrs. Bellinger is sympathetic as the twins tell the story of Johnny's rescue. She rushes into the kitchen to turn off the stove. "Hurry, kids," Mrs. Bellinger said. "We've got to get him to the vet." The four of them jump into the car, and Mrs. Bellinger drives to the nearest veterinarian. When they walk into the office, Johnny recognizes it as a place he has come to before with Hud. "Well hello Johnny!" The vet greets them. "What brings you here?" "Johnny hurt," he responded. Mrs. Bellinger fills the vet in on the events leading to Johnny's rescue. "Well, let's take a look at you," Doc said, as he begins a thorough examination of Johnny, paying particular attention to the bad leg. Upon completion of the examination, the Doctor cleans Johnny up and reports to the trio.

"Johnny will be OK in a few days, just a bad sprain. He will need to take it easy but with lots of TLC he'll be fine, and give my regards to Hud."

As they return to the car, Mrs. Bellinger praises the twins for caring so much about an injured animal. "However," she informs them, "you will need to get your father's permission to keep him. We have to hurry home now, It's almost five o'clock and I have dinner to prepare." Dinner time at the Winters household is always at six o'clock sharp and Mrs. Bellinger takes great pride in being very prompt. "You can talk to your father about Johnny then."

Since the separation of their parents, Amie and Jimmy spend most of their time with their father, Thomas Winters. Most weekends and a portion of the summer are spent with their Mother, Lois Winters. Lois, is a schoolteacher, and lives in Washington, DC. Tom Winters is a FBI Agent. He is a seasoned agent and many times is sent on dangerous missions. Amie and Jimmy are not aware of the dangers of his job. Richard, (Rick), their older brother is currently attending Harvard Law School, and will return home for the summer break in a few days.

The twins talk with Johnny, as the three of them anxiously await their father's arrival. At last, the sound of the car pulling into the driveway alerts them their father is home. They run to the door to greet him and noting their excitement, Tom asked, "What's up with you two?" Then he spies Johnny peering from behind Jimmy's pant leg. "And who might this be?" He asked. "This is Johnny, we found him all beaten up and bleeding." Amie replied.

"We brought him home, and Mrs. Bellinger took us to the veterinarian, where they fixed him up."

"The vet said he needs to rest for a few days. Please, please can we keep him, Daddy?" Jimmy begged. "Just until his owner comes to get him." "And where is his owner?" Tom asked. "He lives on the next street," Amie joins in, "and we left our names and phone number with his landlady. He will call us when he gets home." Mr. Winters looks at the parrot, then at the children, "OK, but some parrots are real loud, and you have to promise to keep him quiet." Mr. Winters smiles, as Johnny promises, "Johnny be quiet."

"We will take very good care of him and we promise he won't make a lot of noise," Jimmy said, as he looks at Johnny now cradled in Amie's arms. She has him wrapped in a pillowcase with his head peeking out looking gratefully at Mr. Winters. "You're safe now and we will take care of you until your owner comes back." Johnny pecks Jimmy gently on the cheek, "Oh thank you, thank you." Mr. Winters heart melts as he watches the twins take Johnny upstairs. They sure are good kids, he thinks, but you never know what to expect with kids. And now a parrot! He chuckles as he goes into the den to work on his computer. Before he begins his work, he calls Mrs. Bellinger, on the intercom. "Can you hold off on dinner for a half hour?" "No problem," she replied. Since their separation, Tom tries to work at home as much as possible. Sitting at his computer, Tom types the names of two individuals, a qualified informant provided earlier in the day. He is alarmed by the information he discovers, and is deep in thought when he hears, Mrs. Bellinger's voice from the kitchen, "Dinner is ready."

Amie places Johnny carefully in the cage, they had found in the attic. The family sits down to a delicious chicken dinner Mrs. Bellinger prepared. Amie, and Jimmy are so excited about being able to keep Johnny, they can't think about anything else, or participate in the family dinner conversation. Dinner over, the twins excuse themselves to spend time with Johnny. They learn more, and more, about each other as they exchange information about their lives.

The Winters family live in a big three-story house on Elm Street in Roseville, Virginia. Amie and Jimmy sleep on the second floor, but their game room that houses their computer is on the third floor. They like it that way, because it's hard for Mrs. Bellinger to climb the steep stairs and they have a lot of privacy. It was decided, Johnny's cage would also go on the third floor. The twins placed the cage in front of the window so that Johnny can have a good view of the neighborhood.

Since it's the beginning of summer and the twins are out of school, Johnny is allowed out of his cage during the daytime. Jimmy is upstairs with Johnny, getting him situated. "Our brother, Rick, will be coming home soon from Law School, just wait till he finds out we have a parrot in our house." "I have another brother?" Johnny exclaimed with excitement.

Jimmy and Amie like to ride their bikes to the beach, which is a little more than a mile from their house. As they climb onto their bikes for their morning ride to the beach, Johnny swoops down from the open window, and lands on the handlebars of Jimmy's bike, "Johnny wants to go to the beach too." Amie looks surprised, and turns to Jimmy. Did you tell him we were going to the beach?" "No. I didn't mention the beach to Johnny, I'm just as surprised as you are."

Looking at Johnny, he asked, "How did you know we were going to the beach?" "That's simple, cause I can read your minds." "That's ridiculous," Jimmy remarked. "Parrots can't read minds." "If you can read minds, what am I thinking right now?" "Hot fudge sundae, hot fudge sundae," Johnny squawked. Jimmy and Amie stare at each other in disbelief. "That was just a lucky guess, bet you can't read my mind," Amie said doubtfully. "Whiz Kid, Whiz Kid," Johnny replied. "This is so cool," Amie exclaimed! "Unbelievable!"

Johnny, perched on the handlebars of Jimmy's bike, suddenly bursts into song, with "A Bicycle Built for Two." The three of them are quite a sight as Amie, and Jimmy join Johnny in song as they ride merrily to the beach.

As they approach the beach, Jimmy cautions Amie, "Johnny's mind reading ability, should be kept a secret between them, and their good friend Whiz. If everyone knew, unscrupulous people might try to kidnap Johnny and we would all be in danger," he warned. The three of them scan the crowd looking for Whiz, whose real name is Alfred Bamett. All of his friends call him Whiz, because he is such a computer whiz.

Like the twins, Whiz is thirteen years of age and attends George Washington, Junior High School in Roseville, Virginia. As they near the Video Arcade, Jimmy spots Whiz showing off his skill at playing video games. Whiz has the reputation of being unbeatable, but this doesn't stop other kids from trying to beat him.

When the game is finished and another defeated challenger leaves the Arcade, Jimmy, and Amie approach the Whiz. "Come on outside," Jimmy said. "We've got something to show you." "Sure," Whiz responded. "We would like to introduce you to our new friend, Johnny the Parrot." Johnny, still perched on the handlebars of Jimmy's bike, takes note of the thoughts going through the Whiz's head, as the three of them approach their bikes. Johnny is eyeing the Whiz and determines he is a good guy. Nothing bad on his mind. "We're taking care of him until his owner comes back from a business trip," Jimmy explained. The Whiz walks up to Johnny, "Hi, pretty bird, glad to meet you." Johnny looks into the Whiz's eyes, "Likewise Dude", he replied. The Whiz, taken aback by Johnny's response, bursts into laughter. "He's quite a bird!"

"You haven't heard anything yet," Amie said. "He is really smart, but if we show you what he can do, you have to promise to keep it a secret." "I swear I won't tell a soul," Whiz vowed. Amie continues talking, "think of something, but don't say it out loud, just look at Johnny."

Johnny stares back at the Whiz, "Sierra, Sierra," he said. "Wow, I was thinking about my girl friend, Sierra. Is this for real? Amazing! He can, really read minds!" "We discovered it on the way to the beach," Jimmy exclaimed. "This is going to be some summer, with Johnny being able to talk and read minds! Think of the fun that we are going to have with him."

The twin's lock their bikes to the bike stand, in front of the video store, and the group heads down to the water with Whiz carrying the surfboard, he had just rented. They remove their shoes and walk briskly along the beach. Amie squeals as the hot sand oozes between her toes. They are all happy to get to the water. The Whiz runs with his surfboard as Jimmy and Amie dive into the water for a swim. "Can I fly around the beach, and see what's happening?" Johnny asked. "Stay close enough where we can see you, we don't want to lose you," Amie cautioned him.

As Johnny glides over the beach, he spots a young couple on a blanket. "What's that their drinking?" he asked as he swoops down to get a closer look. "Well I'll be darned it's beer! A couple sips of beer wouldn't be bad in this hot weather." With that, he comes in for a landing right next to the couple on the blanket. "Hi, my name is Johnny," he squawked. The couple caught by surprise, look at each other, and laughingly the man says, "You sound just like Johnny Carson. Where did you learn to talk so good?" Johnny, anxious to get to the beer, ignores their question. "How about sharing a few sips of your beer?" Johnny asked. Amazed at how well the bird talks the man pours a little beer into a plastic cup. "Let's see what he does with this." Johnny sticks his beak into the cup and gulps the beer. "I've never seen such a bird, no one will believe this when we tell them," the girl exclaimed. Her partner agreed, "a day at the beach has never been more entertaining." Upon finishing the beer Johnny thanked them, and said, "much obliged, it sure hit the spot," and flew off. The couple laughing, but still finding it hard to believe, waved goodbye. "That couple of sips of beer sure tasted refreshing on this hot day. I think I'll fly around the beach, and see if anyone else has some."

"Look there's another beer drinker." He swoops down for a landing, right next to the beer drinking man. "How about sharing your beer with a thirsty bird?" The man surprised, laughed, "sure thing, young man," as he pours some beer into a plastic cup. "Aah that's really good cold beer," Johnny sighed. The stranger pours some more beer into his cup, and hold's up his beer to Johnny, "down the hatch," as they both continue to indulge. It's a little more than Johnny needed and he starts to get a little tipsy.

Looking up at his face, Johnny senses something is wrong and taps immediately into the man's mind. An elderly lady, sitting nearby with some kids, has her purse lying open on their blanket. The man is fantasizing about grabbing the purse; as he is an expert at identity theft. "It would be so easy," he thinks, "the old lady is pretty frail, and by the time she can get up, I'll be long gone.

She can't give me much trouble, she's an easy mark."
Johnny is scared for the old lady. "I know what you're
up to," Johnny screeched at the man. "I'm going to get
my friends, and tell them what you're going to do." As
Johnny flies away, the man grabs the wallet from the purse
and begins to follow him, ignoring the woman's screams
the man follows behind Johnny. "That weird bird can
talk so good, anyone can understand him. I can't have
him telling people what I'm doing." Johnny is in such a
hurry to find Amie, and Jimmy; he doesn't realize he is
being followed. Catching sight of the twins Johnny yells,
"Bad Man—Bad Man." Amie runs over to Johnny, "calm
down, Johnny tell me what's wrong." Johnny tells Amie
about the man's plan to steal the lady's purse. Jimmy
and Whiz run out of the water to see what Johnny is
talking about. They follow Johnny up the beach, but as
they approach the spot where the man was sitting, "he's
gone," Johnny squawked. They continue to look for the
man, but he has disappeared. Unbeknown to the kids,
the man is hiding behind the bathhouse watching their
every move.

It's getting late and the kids have to get home. They
return to the Arcade to pick up their bikes. Johnny, who
is a little tipsy, rides in the basket of Jimmy's bike and
takes a nap. When they get near their house, the Whiz
says goodbye and heads home. The twins and Johnny
still, are not aware they are being followed.

The kids and Johnny go inside, just in time for dinner.
During dinner, they tell their Dad and Mrs. Bellinger

about the day at the beach. Amie begins to tell them about the man, and his thoughts of grabbing the lady's purse. "Hey, wait a minute, how did you know what he was thinking?" Tom asked. "Whoops," Amie said, "we were going to keep that a secret." "Keep what a secret?" Tom asked.

Jimmy begins to tell their Dad about Johnny's ability to read minds. "Go get him and bring him down here, I want to talk to him," Mr. Winters ordered. Jimmy yells at the foot of the stairs. "Johnny, come on down here, Dad wants to talk to you." Johnny, still half-asleep, and not feeling so good, ambles slowly down the stairs.

"Is it true you can read minds?" Mr. Winters demanded. "Think of something, and I'll show you," Johnny replied. Mr. Winters focuses on the apple pie that Mrs. Bellinger has placed on the table. "Apple pie - Apple pie!" Johnny squawked. Mr. Winters stares in disbelief as he gapes at the bird, with his mouth open. "I can't believe this," he said. "WOW! That's exactly what I was thinking."

Mr. Winters, because of his work with the FBI, feels he has seen and heard most everything. Never has he seen anything like Johnny. He and Johnny spend some time talking, while Amie and Jimmy retreat to the living room to watch TV. The more Mr. Winters talks with Johnny, the more impressed he becomes with Johnny and all of his abilities. "We're happy to have you staying with us and I think maybe, you can help me with the twins.

Keep an eye on them for me, meanwhile make yourself comfortable."

"Time for bed kids," Mr. Winters called out. Jimmy turns the TV off, and he and Amie say their good nights to Mrs. Bellinger and their Dad. As they climb the stairs, with Johnny following behind them, he says, "Wait up I don't feel so good I got a head-ache," he moaned. "You're okay, you just have a hangover," Jimmy said. The twins giggle as they finish their walk up the stairs.

Meanwhile, lurking in the dark shadows outside the house, is the man from the beach. He's trying to figure out a way to get into the house and grab Johnny. "That bird has some unusual talents. How else could he know what I was thinking when we were at the beach? I could make a lot of money with him, but I have to figure out a way to get him." Suddenly he spies a ladder the painters had left at the rear of the house. Grabbing the ladder, he carries it around the corner of the house, where he sees the light on the third floor. He places the ladder against the house with Johnny sleeping in full view inside the open window. The man carefully begins the climb up the ladder, trying to be very quiet. He slips on a rung of the ladder, getting Johnny's attention. Johnny immediately wakes up, swoops out of the open window squawking loudly. His wings hit the man's face, causing him to fall off the ladder into the bushes below.

Jimmy and Amie run to the window to see what all of the commotion is about. There, in the bushes, they see a man with Johnny circling over him. Jimmy yells down the stairs, "Dad there's a guy in the bushes outside our window, hurry and get your gun." Mr. Winters is use to moving quickly, grabs his gun, and runs outside. Looking at the man that Johnny is holding captive, Mr. Winters yells, "Don't move! I'm a FBI agent, I have a gun and will use it if I have to. Kids, call 911."

It seems like forever before they hear the sirens blaring down the street, although, it's only been a matter of minutes. The police rush in, and Mr. Winters explains what has happened. The police lieutenant takes one look at the man. "You look awfully familiar, haven't I seen your mug at the station before?" "No," the man answered. "This is all a big mistake. I worked here as a painter and left my tools. Honestly, I just came back for my tools." "How did the ladder get by the window?" Mr. Winters inquired. The intruder mutters, "I guess one of the painters left it here." The lieutenant rolls his eyes, "likely story," he said. "You can tell the rest of your story down at the station. Officer, come over here and read this creep his rights."

Mr. Winters, the twins, and Johnny watch as the police drive away with the suspected thief. "Well that's it for tonight kids, let's get back to bed."

The next morning, the family enjoys a healthy breakfast of Mrs. Bellinger's famous blueberry pancakes and fruit. Johnny is given some blueberries and joins then at the table.

After breakfast, Amie turns on the news just in time to hear the news reporter talking about an arrest on Elm Street. The newscaster reports, "a two-time convicted identity thief was apprehended in Roseville last night, with the help of a parrot. The reporter repeats himself, "that's right, folks, I said with the help of a parrot." He explains, "it seems the bird flew into the man's face, causing him to fall off a ladder, as he was trying to break into the Winters house." The reporter laughs, and comments, "this is a hilarious story, it should make national headlines." Then a picture of the captured man being hauled off to jail is flashed across the screen.

"Bad-man, Bad-man", "that's the man at the beach," Johnny squawked. Jimmy looks at Johnny, "Good Boy, you should get a citizen's award for putting that awful man in jail." "I'd rather have ice cream," Johnny replied. Amie laughs as she rubs Johnny's head. "You are a real character, Johnny."

After breakfast with his family, Tom Winters leaves to go to work, at the FBI headquarters in Washington, DC. He feels comfortable leaving the twins for the day, under the watchful eyes of Johnny. Tom sits down at his computer to continue the investigation he started the night before. He brings up the file of the two men, and gets to work to see what he can find out about them. One of Tom's specialties is his ability to hack into computers. After several attempts, he finally has success tapping into the web-site he has been seeking.

These men are dangerous, he thinks, as he learns more about their activities. Their plan has something to do with this year's election and the removal of the President. Most of the plan is in secret code. I'll have to get some help with this tomorrow. My colleague at the Pentagon should be able to decipher this code.

Unknown to Tom the suspects have a very sophisticated tracking device, and are aware that someone has hacked into their computer, and they know just where it's coming from.

Tom Winters continues gathering all the information he can. He doesn't take time out for lunch, and before he realizes it is almost five o'clock. "I'll have to hurry home if I want to have dinner with my family." Grabbing his briefcase and laptop he hurries to the parking garage.

He is deep in thought as he walks toward his car. So deep in thought, he doesn't notice the big black Cadillac following him. Suddenly, the driver of the Cadillac accelerates, and tires squeal, as the car crashes into Mr. Winters, hurling him into the air. The car speeds off leaving him unconscious on the garage floor.

An office worker, just entering the parking garage, watches the accident in horror. Her screams echo through the parking ramp, as the car had slammed into Mr. Winters. She runs over to him, feeling as though she's frozen in time, although it feels like she's moving in slow motion. If only she had seen what was coming, she could have warned him. Kneeling down beside him she feels his pulse, and detects a faint heartbeat. "Thank heaven he's still alive," at the same time she is frantically digging through her purse to find her cell phone. "There it is," and she quickly dials 911.

The dispatcher answers the call, and the witness tries to remain calm, and speak slowly so that an ambulance can be sent immediately. The dispatcher reassures her that help is on the way. She cautions, "under no circumstances are you to move the injured man. Just remain with him until the ambulance arrives."

Suddenly, she hears the siren as the ambulance approaches. The paramedics jump from the ambulance and quickly check Tom's vital signs. Although in bad shape, they determine he is still alive. One of the paramedics phones the hospital from the accident site, so the hospital can prepare for their arrival, and no time will be lost when they arrive. Tom is put onto a gurney, then into the ambulance and they speed off to the hospital with the sirens blaring full blast.

At home, Mrs. Bellinger receives a call from the hospital informing her of the accident. The nurse states, "Thomas Winters has been injured in a hit and run accident, and the family must come to the hospital immediately."

Rick, the twin's older brother just home from college, takes charge and soon the four of them are driving to the hospital. Upon arrival, they rush into the emergency room. "How's he doing?" Rick asked the nurse on duty.

"The Doctor will be in to see you soon, and will give you a full report on his condition," she replied. Amie, and Jimmy huddle closely to Rick, in an attempt to capture some of his strength. "I'm so glad that you are home Rick," Mrs. Bellinger said. She sees how the twins depend on their older brother.

The Doctor enters the room, and gives the family a brief prognosis. "Your father is in very serious condition, he reported. He has a long fight ahead of him. He's conscious at the moment, but I've given him a sedative. He won't be awake for long, and only two of you can go in at a time." Rick assures the twins, "don't worry everything will be OK."

Rick and Amie walk into his room. Amie flinches at the sight of her Dad covered with bandages, and tubes coming from his body. She kisses him lovingly. Tom attempts to tell them what happened. "I don't think this was an accident." Rick, you need to find my car, and get my laptop, and hide it in a safe place." "Don't worry Dad I'll take care of it." Rick and Amie leave the room, so that Jimmy and Mrs. Bellinger can come in. Soon, Mr. Winters is sleeping, and the Doctor tells them they must leave so he can rest. "Don't worry, we will take excellent care of your Dad," as he pats Jimmy on the shoulder.

Leaving the hospital with their father's personal belongings, Rick looks through his father's wallet, and pockets, searching for clues as to why this happened. He tells the twins, "nothing out of the ordinary here." The four of them pile into Rick's Mustang and head for the Police impound to retrieve their father's laptop. Rick explains who they are to the Sgt., and asks for permission to take his father's laptop from the car. "I'll call down to the guard on duty, and give him the okay for you guys to pick it up at the guard's gate."

On the drive home he asked the twins, "do you have any idea what was going on that would put Dad in such danger? "Dad seemed up tight about something last night. He's spent a lot of time working on his computer," Jimmy answered. At home, Rick gets the laptop and begins to search for any data his Dad might have been working on. He locates the most recent file, and attempts to hack into the files of the suspects. Rick is amazed at the security his Dad has installed in his computer, and even more amazed at the security of the web-site his Dad had been attempting to hack into. After a couple of hours, Rick has to admit he can't do it. He tells the twins, "we need someone smarter than I am, if we're going to hack into that web-site."

Amie and Jimmy look at each other. "Are you thinking what I'm thinking?" Amie asked. "The Whiz kid! He's a genius," Jimmy replied. "If anyone can hack into that computer, it would be him. No one is smarter with computers than he is." "Great," Rick says, "Call him first thing in the morning. Now it's time for you two to go to bed. It has been a long day, and try to get some sleep."

The twins awaken to the sound of Johnny's, "wake up it's morning." They hurry down the stairs, just as Rick hangs up the phone. "That was the hospital," he said. "Dad is holding his own. The best thing we can do for him is to let him rest. The next best thing we can do is figure out a way to hack into that web-site. We need to find out who has caused all this. Is it too early to call the Whiz?" "It's early," Amie replied. "But I know he'll love the challenge!" Amie can tell by the sound of Whiz's groggy voice that the phone woke him up. "Sorry to wake you Whiz, but we've got a problem with our computer, and could use your help." "What time is it?" he asked. "It's seven o'clock," Amie answered. "But this is urgent!" She finally has his attention. "So, you can't figure it out without the Whiz?" "Right." "You know you are the smartest kid in school." "That's what I like to hear," Whiz said. "I'll be right over."

Upon Whiz's arrival the four of them with Johnny perched on Rick's shoulder go into Mr. Winter's computer room. Talking in low voices, so as not to upset Mrs. Bellinger, they fill the Whiz in on the hit and run accident, and their Dad's injuries. "Wow! Is he going to be okay?" Whiz asked. "He's holding his own this morning," Rick answered. "Dad doesn't believe it was an accident. He is pretty sure of who's behind this, and asked us to try and hack into their computer. Man, I'm usually pretty good with computers," Rick continued, "but I didn't have any luck this time." Whiz sits down at the computer. "This might take some time," he said, "but I'll figure it out."

"I have to go to the hospital and see dad," Rick said. "I'll be gone a couple hours." The Whiz continues his effort to hack into their computer, while the twins take Johnny downstairs so as not to disturb the Whiz.

After a few hours, Rick returns from the hospital, hearing Whiz yelling, "I got it!" Rick and the twins rush upstairs, all shouting, "yea, we're in, we're in," as they dance around the room. Johnny echoes, "we're in, we're in."

Unbeknown to the Whiz, the suspects are aware that their system is being hacked into again. They also know that the hacking is coming from Tom Winters' computer. The kids are unaware of the dangers that lie ahead of them.

The four of them decide to call it a day. Most of the day has been spent on the computer. "There is still a lot of work ahead," Whiz informed them, but agrees they should leave it for tomorrow. "Why don't you call your folks and see if you can stay overnight?" Jimmy asked. "You can sleep in my bed, and I'll sleep in the family room, that way, we can get an early start in the morning." "Good idea!" Rick said. With that, the four of them are off to bed. Johnny falls asleep in his cage on the third floor. Soon the house is dark, as one by one, they fall asleep.

Meanwhile, a car pulls up to the curb in front of the Winters' house. The men inside wait patiently, until the lights are out, and they feel confident everyone inside is asleep. Two hours pass, and they agree, "now is the time." One of the two go about the business of picking the lock on the front door, as the other guy keeps watch for anyone approaching on the street. Within seconds, they are in the entryway of the house. The men proceed cautiously, as they climb up the stairs to Jimmy's room.

The pair quickly open the bedroom door, sees the kid in bed, who they believe is Jimmy Winters. The Whiz stirs just before duct tape is slapped across his mouth. Now awake, but unable to scream he squirms as the men quickly grab a blanket, and tie it around him.

The two men carry Whiz, quietly downstairs, and grab their Dad's computer. As they are leaving one of the men flicks his cigarette lighter and sets fire to the drapes.

Outside, the men throw Whiz into the trunk of their car, and speeds down the street. Whiz meanwhile, trying to remain cool, is secretly terrified as he twists and turns, trying to free himself from the blanket. "Stay cool," he mumbled through the duct tape. "This is an adventure, and I have to have confidence I can escape somehow." His cockiness returns and Whiz thinks, "Somehow I can outwit these thugs, after all I am the Whiz."

Jimmy, sleeping in the family room, wakes up to the smell of smoke. He jumps up, grabs the fire extinguisher, and tries to put the fire out, but to no avail. The fire has spread quickly. Jimmy yells, "Fire, Fire" as he runs into Mrs. Bellinger's room. "Call 911, the house is on fire." Mrs. Bellinger grabs the phone next to her bed and quickly dials 911.

Jimmy races up the stairs still shouting, "Fire, Fire." Amie and Rick jump out of bed. "Amie get out of the house now," Rick barked. "Jimmy, get the Whiz and I'll get Johnny." Jimmy runs into his room to wake up the Whiz. No Whiz! He must have already left the house, Jimmy thinks as he runs to the den to grab his Dad's computer. The computer is gone too! "Rick, the Whiz is gone and so is Dad's computer," Jimmy yelled. Jimmy, Rick and Johnny leave the house to join Amie and Mrs. Bellinger who are already outside. They can hear the sirens of the fire trucks coming down the street.

Everyone is waiting outside when the firemen arrive. They set about trying to extinguish the flames. Soon, the fire is out with only the front of the house badly burned.

The rest of the house has smoke and water damage. "Is everyone accounted for here?" one of the firemen asked. "We can't find our friend, Alfred Barnett," Rick replied.

The firemen immediately begin to search the house trying to locate the Whiz. Finding no sign of him, the firemen call the police, and gather information to file a missing person report. The police asked Rick, for a detailed description of Whiz. They also notify Whiz's parents of their son's disappearance, and request they furnish a current picture of him. Soon after, an Amber Alert is posted.

The neighbors are gathered outside to see what the commotion is about. Mrs. Hunt, who lives next door to the Winters, spots Rick, and rushes over to him, "thank God you are okay." "Where is the rest of your family?" She asked. "Everyone got out safely, but our friend Whiz is missing." A thorough search of our house has been completed, and he has not been accounted for." Mrs. Hunt has a worried look on her face, "oh my." Rick cut her off in the middle of her sentence. "What's wrong?" he asked. "When I was walking my dog Peaches, I noticed a black car parked in the street with the motor running. I was suspicious of the car because it was still parked in the street when I returned from my walk. I hid behind the bushes, and luckily I had a pen and paper with me and jotted down the license plate number." She hands Rick a piece of paper with the plate number on it, "and that's not all, this is the most frightening part of what I saw, they put something big and squirming into their trunk."

Rick has a worried look on his face, "that was probably the Whiz, this is not good." Rick takes the plate number and walks over to where the police are standing, and hand's the paper to one of them. He tells the policeman what Mrs. Hunt had observed. "My Dad is Thomas Winters. He works for the FBI, and he and Lt. Bill Boyd have worked together on crime cases. Can you pass this information onto the Lt. as soon as possible?"

The policeman assures Rick, that he will forward the license plate number to the Lt.

Rick is thinking to himself, I need to get my family away from here, it is not safe. He pulls out his cell phone, and calls his mother who lives in DC. Rick tells her about the fire, and Whiz's kidnapping. "Are the twins all right?" she asked. "Yes they are fine," Rick answered. They are both very scared and worried about their friend Whiz." "Hurry and get to my house as soon as possible. Bring Mrs. Bellinger and Johnny too. I will be waiting for you and drive safely."

On the drive to their Mother's, Rick tells everyone about what Mrs. Hunt had seen, and now Amie who had been calm, is really upset, and crying. Jimmy is in the back seat hugging her. Rick stops for a red light, and turns around and squeezes her hand. "We are going to find Whiz, we just have to think positive, and trust the authorities will find Whiz alive and well." The light turns green and Rick speeds off with Amie's sobs subsiding. Mrs. Bellinger is reassuring Amie that everything is going to work out.

They no sooner, get Amie calmed down when Jimmy started moaning, "if only I had been in my own bed, Whiz would not have been kidnapped." Now it is Amie's turn to comfort Jimmy, "that's ridiculous, then it would have been you." Rick chimes in, "hey guys let's not put the blame on anyone. What we need to do is figure out a way to get to the bottom of this." Rick continues talking to the twins; nothing is going to happen to Whiz. I'll tell you just what I just got through telling Amie, the police will find him no matter what it takes." Johnny is squawking in the back seat, "find Whiz, find Whiz." The twins feel better, and agree with their older brother, Whiz will be found unharmed.

It is late when they arrive at their Mother's house. Mrs. Winters hugs and kisses her children. She can see that they are a little shaken, but they are okay. "Let's go into the kitchen, for some hot chocolate." They sit around the kitchen table talking about the fire, and Whiz's kidnapping. Mrs. Winters does her best to reassure her children that everything will work out. Finally seeing her family has calmed down, and their hot chocolate finished, Mrs. Winters says, in an upbeat tone, "c'mon kids let's go to bed, and I promise you everything will look brighter in the morning."

The next morning Rick drives to the hospital, while the twins are still sleeping. He approaches his Dad's room, and sees two armed guards standing in front of the door. Rick is asked to show his ID before he is allowed to enter. As he enters, Tom Winters opens his eyes, "hi son." Rick gives his Dad a hug, and relates to him about the events of the last twenty-four hours. "Dad you have to tell me what the heck is going on." "You are right son I didn't realize the investigation that I am working on would involve my family. I am so sorry the Whiz is missing, his parents must be frantic." Tom's voice is sounding weaker, and Rick can tell he is getting tired. "Listen carefully Rick, the men I have been investigating work at the White House, and the information I have gathered concerning them is on my laptop. I don't want to place you in any further danger, but you have to turn my computer over to my reliable friend, Ray Perron, a fellow FBI agent. I would trust him with my life.

He'll know what to do next." "Sorry Dad, the guys that set the house on fire took your computer along with Whiz." Tom takes a deep breath, "this is worse than I thought. Rick, write down the names of Jack Thorton , and Harry Morgan." While Rick is writing this down, Tom also gives him Ray Perron's telephone number.

Tom drifts back to sleep, as Rick goes outside to call Ray. He fills him in about all of the events that have occurred. Rick also gives him the license plate number of the black car for Ray to check out. Ray says, "I was up to see your Dad this morning, but he was asleep, so I didn't disturb him. I will get to work on this, and see what I can find out. Meanwhile please be careful, I'm not sure what these thugs are up to."

Rick drives back to his Mother's house, and tells the family how their father is doing. The twins are relieved their Dad is doing better. Jimmy asks, "when can we go to see him?" Rick answers, "It will be awhile, he needs his rest, and the hospital will call to let us know when he is strong enough to have visitors." Tears well up in Amie's eyes, and Rick says, "don't worry Dad's going to be just fine, it's just going to take awhile. Why don't you and Jimmy get on Mom's computer, and make him a special greeting card." "Good idea, c'mon Jimmy let's get busy."

Rick's phone rings and it is Ray Perron. He tells Rick, "the black Cadillac, was reported stolen yesterday, from the White House parking garage. So far this is the only information I have for you, but when I find out anything else I'll call you back." Rick says, "I appreciate you calling with this up-date and hope to be talking to you soon."

The kids and Johnny are trying to get settled down at their Mother's. They have finished the greeting card, and placed it on the mantle to take with them when they are allowed to visit their Dad.

Johnny and Amie are sharing a bedroom. Johnny cannot go anywhere, so he has been watching TV and enjoying it. Every time someone comes into his room, he says, "hi Dude." This is an expression he picked up from the TV awhile back and in spite of everything that has happened, he makes everyone laugh.

Mrs. Winters, and Mrs. Bellinger decide to take the twins to the mall. They both agree that keeping the twins busy will help take their minds off their missing friend, and their father's accident. When they left the burning house they only had the clothes on their back, so it is a necessity to take them shopping for clothes and other things they will need.

Neither twin wanted to leave the house, in case news came about their friend, and if the hospital should call about their father. Mrs. Winters tells them, "you don't have to worry, if I receive any calls on my home phone it automatically transfers to my cell phone, so we won't miss any calls. Grab your jackets and let's go."

Now that everyone has left, Rick sits down at his Mother's computer, and types the words White House, and clicks onto the Personnel Department. He is surprised how easy it is to find the addresses, of the two names his father had given him. Rick decides to try and hack into the Department of Motor Vehicles, and get the license plate numbers, and the make of the vehicles, for Harry Morgan and Jack Thorton. He waits a few minutes for the information to finally appear on the monitor. He jots this down in his notebook and logs off the computer.

When the twins return from their shopping trip, Rick takes them aside, and tells them what he found out. The three of them decide to drive to the parking garage of the White House, to see if they can get lucky, and locate Harry Morgan and Jack Thorton's cars. Rick tells their Mom, they are going for ice cream. They arrive at the parking garage and find a good place to park, and settle down to wait, as they watch every car that comes and goes.

About two hours go by, the car owned by Harry Morgan, pulls out of the parking garage. Rick quickly starts his Mustang, and hangs back a few cars to follow him. Rick yells back to the twins, "help me keep an eye out, the traffic is heavy and I don't want to lose this guy." "Sure thing, we won't let you lose sight of him," Jimmy answers, as his eyes are firmly planted on Morgan's car. Amie says, "oh I hope he leads us to the Whiz." Jimmy answers her without taking his eyes off the suspect's car. "We probably won't be that lucky, but we may get some clues as to where the Whiz is."

They follow Harry Morgan for a few miles, when he pulls into the parking lot of Howard's restaurant and bar. He quickly walks into the bar looking back over his shoulder to see if he is being followed. Rick tells the twins. "Wait on the restaurant side and have some ice cream." Rick then walks into the bar side and orders a coke. He sits as close as he can to the table where Harry Morgan is setting. After a few minutes, another man comes in and sits down. Rick can hear one of the men asking the other, "what are we going to do with the kid?" When Rick hears that, he knows they are on the right track, they have to be talking about the Whiz he says to himself. Rick hurriedly goes into the restaurant side to retrieve the twins, and pays for their ice cream.

They go back to their car to wait for the men to come out. The men finally leave the bar and get into separate cars and leave. Rick decides to follow Harry Morgan, with hopes he might lead him to Whiz. Rick sees a clearing and gets in line to exit the parking lot. Morgan is about five car lengths ahead of them as they head toward the busy marina. Cars are pulling in and out of traffic, and they quickly lose track of their suspect. Darn, Rick mumbles, "we've lost him." Jimmy remarks, "this marina looks like a maize. We are never going to find him in this mess." Rick says, "your right, but I have a good idea, we'll come back tomorrow with Johnny. He can fly around the marina and look for Morgan's car, and he will be able to fly places we can't go." "What a good idea. Johnny will be able to peek in windows without raising suspicion from these thugs," Amie exclaims excitedly. Rick turns the car around and they head for home.

Unknown to the trio, they were so close to where Whiz is kept prisoner. He is blindfolded, bound and gagged, and held captive in a locked cabin on a fishing boat at the marina. The Whiz strangely enough is not afraid. He sees this as another challenge or a puzzle for his brain to solve. The best asset he has for this difficult predicament, is his confidence he will find a way out. The men assigned to watch the Whiz, also comment about this kid being calm. A little too calm to suit them. Meanwhile the Whiz listens for clues to discover where he is being held. "I think I may be at the marina because of the movement of the boat, and I can hear birds that sound like seagulls." Whiz has been at the marina many times with his parents, and remembers the smell of fish in the air.

To pass away time, he starts thinking about one of the video games he has played, called Kidnapper, he was unbeatable at it. He is thinking about how he could always outsmart his fantasy kidnappers. That's it I will have to outsmart these idiots. That should be easy, given the brain I have, it will be a piece of cake.

The next morning Rick calls Ray Perron, the FBI agent, and tells him about the two men, and the conversation he overheard at the bar. We followed one of the men to the marina and lost him there." Ray cautions Rick, "do not make contact with them, they are very dangerous characters. I know you are anxious for your friend to be found, but let us handle it. I appreciate your leads, but we do not want to place you or your siblings in any danger. Besides, your father would be very angry with me if anything happened to you." "Got it," Rick says.

The three kids, and Johnny, get in Rick's red Mustang and drive to the hospital. Johnny stays in the car, while the kids go in to see their Dad. He is a little bit better, but not out of danger yet. There is a very attractive lady in the room talking to their Dad. She introduces herself as Christine Casey, another FBI agent, and friend of their Father. She explains, "I am one of the agents working on the kidnapping of Alfred Barnett. Have you heard anything more about the case," she asks Rick. Rick reports to her the same information that he had given Ray Perron. The kids spend a couple hours with their Dad, and after Christine left, Tom says, "Christine is a very good detective and a good friend." They say their good-byes, and give their Father a hug, and walk back to Rick's car, where Johnny is waiting. Johnny says, "hi, how's your Dad," the trio bursts out laughing, Jimmy says, "thanks for asking he is getting better and is no longer in intensive care."

Johnny looks at him with his big eyes, and says, "super dude. It's three o'clock in the afternoon. Rick says, "let's go stake out the entrance to the marina. Maybe with Johnny's help we can get lucky and find the Whiz. You guys, stay in the car while I look around." As he walks through the Marina, he says to himself, wow there must be a thousand boats in here.

Rick returns to his car, as Jimmy is saying excitingly, "that black car of Harry Morgan's just went by." "Okay boy, we need your help now," Rick tells Johnny. "Fly around the Marina and see if you can find the black car." Johnny replies, "gotcha boss," as he flies off. After he has been flying around about twenty minutes, he spots the black car, and lands on the railing of the boat, next to the car. He walks around the railing looking in all the portholes. In one of the windows he sees two men talking. In the next window he spots the Whiz. Whiz does not see Johnny because he is blindfolded. Whiz is still trying to figure out a way to get free of his captors, without getting killed in the process.

Johnny is excited about finding the Whiz. It seems like forever before he gets back to the car. When he gets back to the kids he is breathing really hard, the kids can hardly understand him. Johnny says in a frantic voice, "I found the Whiz, he is alive." Rick pets the top of Johnny's head saying, "good job Johnny you are amazing." After Johnny catches his breath, Rick asks Johnny, "what else did you see?" Johnny describes the boat, the location and the two scary looking men on the boat guarding the Whiz.

Rick tells Johnny to show us what boat the Whiz is on. Rick drives into the marina with Johnny's direction. After a few minutes, Johnny hollers, 'that's the boat the Whiz is on right there." Rick drives a hundred feet or so past the boat and parks. He takes out a pen and paper, and jots down the slip number the boat is docked at.

Rick dials Ray Perron's number from his cell phone and tells him the news. Ray says, "don't do anything, I will handle it from here." He says again, " I mean it, I don't want you kids in any danger. Don't do anything and get out of there right now."

Ray immediately calls for the Swat team. Ray and the Swat team arrive about the same time at the marina. They set up positions on three sides of the boat. The Coast Guard covers the waterside. Ray tells the Swat Captain, "these men are to be captured alive, as they have valuable information I need for the case I am working on." A few minutes later one of the two men is about to leave the boat, when there is a gunshot heard, and the man falls to the deck of the boat. The other man hears the shot and dives into the water. Ray Perron shouts out, "I said no shooting."

Ray runs onto the fishing boat and breaks into the locked cabin. As he sees the Whiz, he unties him and takes off the blindfold, and duct tape. Whiz says, "free at last." Ray asks him, " are you okay?" Whiz replies, " what took you so long? I was really getting worried about getting out of this mess. At first I thought I could figure a way out, but they were guarding me so close it was impossible to free myself." Ray tells him I am impressed with the way you handled yourself in this dangerous situation. Whiz asks Ray, " can I use your cell phone to call my parents?"

Whiz calls his parents. They are frantic with worry, and both are on the phone talking at the same time asking if he is hurt. "I am fine, but the police are sending me to the hospital for observation. Meet me there and you can see for yourself." Ray asks Whiz, "would you like to see your friends, they are just down the street." "Would I ever, he replies." As they walk to Rick's car, Ray says, "it was your friends that found you." "I knew they would come through they are great friends." When they reach the car, the Winters family gives Whiz a big hug. Whiz thanks them for finding him, and Rick says, "it was really Johnny that found you, he discovered which boat you were on." Whiz gives Johnny a big bear hug, and thanks him too. Whiz looks a little embarrassed at all the attention he is getting, and is trying to act cool, by telling the kids, "you know it was just a matter of time before I would have found a way out." "We know, you are one smart dude," Rick says. Ray tells the group, "we need to take Mr. Barnett to the hospital now." Rick asks, "can we can take him?" "Okay," Ray says, "I will follow behind you, I need to get a statement from him when we get to the hospital. Wait for me before you leave, I have to meet with the Swat team Captain."

Ray tells the Captain, "I want all of your men to take a gun powder test to find out which Swat team member fired the fatal shot, and get back to me as soon as possible. They were instructed not to shoot." The Captain replies, "yes sir." Ray asks him, "what happened to the man who jumped overboard?" "We have done an extensive search for him, but we can find no sign of him."

The Whiz meets his parents at the hospital, where, there is a very exciting reunion between the three, as they hug and kiss, and the Whiz tells his parents about the Winters kids, and Johnny rescuing him.

Rick says, "we are going to visit our dad now, and we'll talk to you later.

As they get to their dad's room, there are two armed guards posted at his door, which again reminds them of the danger around them. The twins tell their dad about the exciting rescue of Whiz. Amie says, "it was Johnny that found the boat the bad guys had the Whiz hidden on." Tom shakes his head and says, "I am very proud of you kids, of the way you did everything in your power to help your friend. I am relieved to hear about Whiz, but very disappointed about the two men I have been investigating."

Ray Perron and Christine Casey enter Tom's room and Ray tells him, "the missing man is Jack Thorton, and the man that died is Harry Morgan. The Swat team member who shot Harry Morgan has been identified as Steve Raymond. He has clammed up, but we will interview him some more tomorrow. He'll talk they always do."

The kids get home in time for supper. Their mother and Mrs. Bellinger are very happy the Whiz was rescued, and he is okay. Amie says, "we found him with Johnny's help." Mrs. Winters asked, "how in the world did Johnny help?" Rick says, "we told him what the car looked like and he flew around the marina, until he found it. He then led us to the spot where the car was parked, and we called Ray Perron at the FBI." Mrs. Bellinger says, "you kids might just as well tell her the rest of the story."

Jimmy and Amie tell their mother about finding Johnny, then discovering his mind reading abilities. Their mother says, "what a wonderful gift, if you use it right you will be able to do a lot of good in this world." The kids are very pleased by what their mother said about Johnny.

After they eat, Amie explains to their mother about the incident at the beach, and Johnny reading the mind of someone who was about to commit a crime.

Within this conversation, she tells her mom, "that was where Johnny had met the man who broke into our house." Johnny hears this and says, "good beer - "bad man." Mrs. Winters asks with concern, "what is Johnny talking about when he says good beer?" Amie replies "beer is one of Johnny's favorite treats, and the bad man at the beach gave Johnny some, and he got a little tipsy." Mrs. Winters says to the kids, "I read that alcohol is not good for parrots, and could even kill him. Amie, why don't you go into the den, and see what you can find out about this on the Internet."

Amie has Johnny perched on her shoulder, and the two of them sit down at the computer. She finds the web site, and reads about the foods they should be feeding Johnny. Also included is a warning of food and drinks a parrot should not consume. At the top of the list is a big warning that reads, "do not EVER give a parrot ALCOHOL."

Amie looks at Johnny and says, "that's why you were so sick after you drank beer at the beach." Johnny squawks," I sure don't like the sound of this, beer is my favorite treat." Amie says, "too bad Johnny, you have to promise never to drink beer again, it might kill you." Johnny flies off Amie's shoulder and thinks about it for a minute. " I sure don't want to get sick and die. Okay, I promise, I will never drink beer again, and my second favorite treat is ice cream."

Amie and Johnny return to the family room with Johnny back on her shoulder. Johnny is singing, "no more beer for Johnny, I could get sick and die - sick and die." Mrs. Winters smiles. "Johnny you are a real character," as the rest of the family laughs.

Mrs. Winters is more then a little curious, about Johnny's mind reading. Johnny she asks, "when did you find out you could read minds?" "When I was a little guy in the jungle, trappers took my mother and I was left alone. They were trying to catch me too, but I could outsmart them because I could read their minds, and tell which way they were going. But one day they outsmarted me by putting grapes in a cage, I was real hungry, and there I was trapped."

"The trappers brought me to the United States, and sold me to the pet store where Hud bought me. People would come into the pet shop and look at me, but most of the time I would act up, because I didn't like the way they were thinking. One day Hud came into the store to buy food for his fish, and I knew by reading his mind that he was a good guy. If I wanted this man to be my master, I would have to act real cute, smart, and charming to get his attention. I started saying, hey mister, why don't you take me out of here, and go get a beer, and pizza," and I continued hamming it up. Hud looked at me and roared with laughter. He asked the shop owner the price, and away we went. Mrs. Winters says, "what a fascinating story; I'm glad he bought you."

The next day the trio decides to stake out the house where the swat man, Steve Raymond lives. The kids are aware the FBI is also there. They have to keep a low profile, so the Federal agents don't spot them. They know if they are seen they will make them leave. Luckily there is a park across the street from the apartment building, and the kids will be able to mingle in with the other families. They all have on sunglasses and hats to change their appearance. The chances of the FBI seeing them are slim. The kids know with Johnny's mind reading abilities, they have an advantage over the agents.

Mrs. Bellinger had prepared a picnic lunch for them, and they settle down to wait. They eat their lunch and begin the wait for the man to come out of the building.

Johnny is enjoying being outside, and watches for the man to come out. The kids get a little bored from the long wait, but finally Johnny sees the man and squawks "bad man-bad man." The kids grab their picnic supplies and scurry to their car, as the man is driving off. The FBI also sees the man leave, and the kids are right behind them. Rick tucks his Mustang in behind the agent's car, and blends in with traffic. Steve Raymond is unaware of the caravan that is following him.

After a long drive, and fighting heavy traffic they manage to keep Steve Raymond's car in sight as they end up at the city zoo. They follow him into the parking lot, and park a few rows behind. Rick tells Johnny, "fly ahead so we don't lose him," as Rick grabs his camera, and the three of them hurry to catch up.

Johnny flies back to the kids, lands on Rick's shoulder and says, "the bad man is waiting in line at the entrance." The kids hurry to get in line, and are just a few people behind Steve Raymond. Rick talks in a low tone, and tells Johnny, "keep the man in view while we buy tickets to enter the zoo."

At last they are inside the zoo compound. Johnny yells at the kids, "walk faster, the man is at the bird sanctuary." They stand back and witness him meeting another man. The man is handing Steve Raymond a small envelope, and the other man walks away. Then they see the FBI agents move in, and yell at Steve Raymond "put your hands up, you are under arrest." The agents cuff him and they take him away for questioning.

The kids are ready to leave, they look around for Johnny, but he is nowhere in sight. Rick yells for Johnny, but Johnny doesn't hear him. Rick tells the twins, "go in one direction and I will go in the other, and meet back here in fifteen minutes." They look everywhere, but Johnny is not to be spotted.

Johnny is having such a good time flying around the bird sanctuary; he loses track of time, and forgets his orders from Rick to stay in view of him. Seeing all of these birds bring back memories of when he was living in the jungle, except the birds in the jungle were free. He thinks to himself, at least these birds don't have to worry about being mistreated or go hungry. All the other parrots are staring at Johnny, as he is flying to and fro singing outloud, an old Frank Sinatra song, " Come Fly With Me." It's quite comical to hear Johnny sing, because he makes up most of the lyrics, but he loves to sing. He sees the most beautiful girl parrot in the back of the sanctuary. She is red and yellow, with a spot of turquoise. She looks a lot like Johnny, only with a girlish look. He picks the lock on the door of the cage, and flies in with all the other parrots.

His intention is to meet the parrot at the back of the birdcage that caught his eye. Johnny flies over to her and says, " hi cutie my name is Johnny, can you talk." "Yes of course I can talk, and my name is Barbie." Johnny hops on the swing with Barbie, and it becomes love at first sight.

Meanwhile the kids are searching the area, looking high and low with no luck. They have never seen so many parrots, but they all seem to be having a good time. They are yelling Johnny's name as loud as they can, finally from the back of the cage, Johnny hears his name. He flies over to the side of the cage, and says to Rick; "I'm over here with this beautiful girl parrot named Barbie."

Rick says, "you scared us half to death. I'm glad you have found a girl friend, but we have to go." Johnny tries to leave, but he can't get the cage door open from the inside. They have a security lock on the inside; it seems they have had other parrots that could pick locks. Rick tells Johnny, "quit fooling around, we have to leave." Johnny says to Rick, "I liked to boss, but I can't get the door open." Rick says, "stay put, I will go get a Zookeeper." Johnny flies back to Barbie, and says, "as soon as the zookeeper comes I will have to go, but I will be back soon." They both coo at each other, and are glad to have a little more time together.

Rick locates the twins and motions for them to come over where he is. They come running and excitedly ask, "did you find Johnny?" Rick answers, "Johnny is fine, but he got himself locked up in that large birdcage, and can't get it unlocked from the inside. You two stay here while I go find the zookeeper to get him out of there." The twins are relieved that Johnny is OK.

Rick finds the office and tells the person on duty, "my parrot got into the bird sanctuary and can't get out." "How in the world is that possible, we check those cages every day? If he can get in, then some of the birds probably got out." Rick doesn't dare, tell the attendant about Johnny being able to pick locks.

Rick says, "somehow he found a small gap in the wire, and squeezed in." The zookeeper says, "I don't know how, but we will to do an inspection." The attendant grabs his keys, "let's go get him out of there." They go back to the cage. The attendant opens the door, as Rick yells, "Johnny come out of there." He hears Rick and gives Barbie a hurried peck on the cheek, and says, "I will be back."

Johnny is still perched on Rick's shoulder, as he is chattering away, telling him all about Barbie. He asked the kids, "will you bring me back to visit Barbie?" They all chime in, "Johnny's in love." Rick says, "it is okay with me, but from now on, we will have to get permission from the zoo attendant." Johnny is elated, and is already planning his next visit with his girlfriend.

The next day the kids travel the short distance to the hospital, to visit their Dad. The FBI agents, Ray Perron and Christine Casey are also there. Rick and Ray talk about the arrest yesterday at the zoo. Ray tells Rick, "Steve Raymond is the SWAT team member that we took in for interrogation, and he is not talking. However, we do have a break in the case, we discovered the identity of the other man as George Stiles. We now have him under surveillance. Hopefully, this will give us some further information."

Tom says, "I should be home in a couple of weeks, and then maybe I can find out something about these men." Ray tells them, "we are going to find out who George Stiles knows in the White House."

He goes on to tell Tom and the kids, "do not use your computers anymore, as these men are very dangerous and computer savvy." The kid's stay about an hour then Rick tells his dad, "we had better head for home." Christine says, "we have arranged for you kids to be followed by our men at all times until this is cleared up. These people know who you are, and we need to protect you." Rick says, "thank you, I have to admit that I have been a little nervous since all of this started happening."

The kids get into Rick's red Mustang and head home. They are talking about everything that has been going on. "I wonder what we can do to help." Jimmy says

Amie says, "I have been reading a spy magazine, and in the back of the book, there is an advertisement about these little surveillance bugs you can buy. They are about the size of a dime, and you can stick them on any surface." Rick asks, "do you know the distance the bugs can transmit?" Amie replies, "I believe the ad said fifty miles." Rick says, "that's perfect mom's house is about twenty miles from the White House. Now all we have to do is to think up a plan to plant the bugs in the White House without being seen."

Amie says, "I have it all figured out, our school's summer trip is coming up next week." Jimmy pipes up and says, "YA perfect, that's right, our class is going to the White House for a tour. No one is going to pay attention to a bunch of kids and we can place the bugs in a lot of different locations." Amie says, "I will make reservations tomorrow." Rick says, "and I'll order the bugs by overnight express." Rick also cautions the twins, "we have a very good plan, but if you two are caught, just say you are playing a practical joke." Jimmy tells Rick, "don't worry we won't be caught."

Ray Perron and Christine Casey leave the hospital together. Ray says, "we need to go back and interrogate Steve Raymond. Steve acts scared, and maybe now that some time has passed he will talk. First thing tomorrow morning, we'll both go in and talk to him, and try to get to the bottom of what he is afraid of." "Good plan," Christine says. "I'll see you in the morning."

The next day, the two of them go to the holding cell where Steve Raymond is being held. Christine starts out by asking the man; "do you love your family?" Steve Raymond replies in a raspy voice, "of course I do." Ray interrupts, "your family is in real danger. These people, whoever they are, know you have been arrested. They will do whatever they have to, to shut you up; they are very dangerous people." Steve Raymond puts his head in his hands for quite awhile, and is visibly upset. Christine and Ray look at each other, and they know he is ready to talk.

They wait about fifteen minutes finally Steve looks up; he clears his throat, and says, "the last thing I wanted, was for my family to get involved." He goes on to explain, "a couple of days ago, when I got out of work, there was a man waiting by my car with a gun, and told me to get in and drive. He said he would give me twenty thousand dollars, to take care of the men that kidnapped the wrong kid, and hid him out at the marina. He also threatened my family. I felt like, I didn't have a choice but to go ahead and do as I was told. When I dropped him off I watched him get into a car, and jotted down the license plate number. I swear to God that's all I know." Christine says, "the FBI will protect your family, but you will be charged with the shooting death of Harry Morgan." Steve Raymond gets up to return to his cell, and thanks the agents for taking care of his family. "I wish I had handled things differently, and I am very sorry about what has happened."

Amie phones the Whiz, and asks, "do you want to go on the school's field trip, to the White House next week?" Whiz's answered, "after getting kidnapped at your house, my parents have grounded me from hanging around with you and Jimmy. I won't mention this to my parents that you and Jimmy are going on this tour, and I'll get my permission slip from school next week." Amie replies, "great, because we have some great plans when we get to the White House." Whiz asks, "are you going to get me kidnapped again?" They both laugh and Amie replies, "no, nothing like that, we'll tell you all about it when we see you next week."

Johnny has been restless since he met Barbie at the zoo and says, "I can't get Barbie off my mind." "Don't worry, we are going to the zoo on Saturday, and that's only three days away," Amie says. Johnny flaps his wings with excitement. "I'm going to fly around the neighborhood, and I'll be back in a little while." "Okay, but stay out of trouble and don't be gone a long time."

Johnny flies out the bedroom window that Jimmy has left open for him. Oh good, the next door neighbor's dog is out in his fenced in back yard. I'm going to fly down to see if he is friendly. Johnny thinks to himself, this dog is a little odd; I have seen him twirling around in circles in his back yard chasing his tail. I have heard the neighbors call him Jake. He looks like a white miniature pig, but Amie told me he is a bull terrier. Johnny flies down to the dog, and says, "hi, my name is Johnny." Jake looks up at the parrot, and thinks, am I hearing right, "it sounds like that bird is talking to me." "That's right, I can talk, and I can read your mind too, so keep on thinking, and we'll have a lot of fun this afternoon."

Johnny asks, "is anyone home?" Jake thinks back, he remembers his people have gone to work. Johnny says, "great, let's go in and find some snacks." He follows Jake in through the doggie door, and says, "I know how to open the refrigerator door, with a dishtowel wrapped around the handle." Johnny grabs a dishtowel that is on the kitchen counter, and twists it around the handle of the refrigerator and like magic the door opens. Meanwhile Jake is visualizing that nice ham Mrs. Dubay put in the refrigerator last night. Johnny shoves the ham out of the refrigerator and it lands on the floor. Jake immediately starts eating it. When Johnny pushed the ham out of the refrigerator, he knocked a bottle of red wine, onto the kitchen floor. It broke and made a real mess. Johnny says, "WHOOPS." He quickly grabs the grapes and shuts the refrigerator door. Johnny and Jake track through the wine and head into the living room, onto the beautiful white carpet. When they finish eating, Johnny says, "I'm going back to the kitchen to see if I can find some ice cream." He finds some strawberry ice cream and yells to Jake, "come and help me get the ice cream to the living room." What a sight it is, to see the two of them maneuvering the half-gallon of ice cream into the living room. They eat most of it, and what they didn't eat, melts onto the carpeting along with the wine stains, they had tracked in. What a mess the two of them made.

Johnny hears the front door open. "I had better get out of here" and leaves through the doggie door before Mrs. Dubay sees him. Mrs. Dubay walks into the living room, and sees the mess, and boy does she start hollering at Jake. "How in the world did you get the refrigerator door open?" Mrs. Dubay sees all of the wine tracks on the white carpeting and the empty strawberry ice cream carton.

Along with the dog tracks, there is what looks like bird tracks, "I wonder how a bird got in here Mrs. Dubay screams." Jake thinks to himself, I wish I could tell her, Johnny the parrot did most of the damage.

Johnny flies home as fast as he can. He can still hear Mrs. Dubay yelling at poor Jake. Johnny lands on Mrs. Winters window sill. "Whew, that was a close call. I don't think I want that woman hollering at me." Johnny is feeling a little guilty about leaving Jake to face the music by himself, but not guilty enough to go back. That woman is a little scary. He also thinks to himself, it's a good thing Jake can't talk, or I would be dead meat. I better lay low for a few days until Mrs. Dubay cools off.

Everyone has gathered around the dining room table, to enjoy the home cooked meal, prepared by Mrs. Bellinger. Mrs. Winters asks, "how was everybody's day," they all say fine. Amie asks Rick, "how is dad," as Rick was at the hospital most of the day. He replies, "dad is going to be transferred to a secret location for physical therapy. He will probably be sent somewhere with-in the government, where he can be protected, and receive the best care, and they say they will make him as good as new. Our visits are going to be limited, and pre-arranged by the government, this is set-up to protect dad, and also to protect all of us." Rick goes onto remind everyone, "we are all being followed by FBI agents for our protection too."

Amie starts crying. Mrs. Winters hugs her and reinforces, "we all have to be brave, while this is going on."

After supper the twins, and Johnny, go to the den to watch TV. Johnny is hoping that no one finds out he messed up Mrs. Dubay' s house. He is deep in thought when the news comes on. He looks up as the press secretary Robert Steven's, is giving a speech about the local schools, that will be visiting the White House next week, and they will be giving these schools, special tours. The President will also be there to meet the children. Mr. Stevens is also talking about the up and coming presidential election. Johnny is watching the man talk, and is getting very agitated. Johnny yells at the kids, "the man talking is having bad thoughts about hurting the President. He doesn't want our President to win the election, and wants a man by the name of Robert Ferris, to be elected President." Amie asked, Johnny "are you sure?" Johnny answers excitedly; "yes he really wants to harm the President." Amie says, "WOW this is very serious; we had better let dad know right away."

The next morning the kids go visit their dad, for the last time at the hospital, as he is scheduled to be transferred to Walter Reed. Rick tells their dad what Johnny discovered on TV last night." Tell Johnny, great job. I knew from the time we found out Johnny could read minds, he would be a valuable asset to us. This is the break we need to get to the bottom of this situation." Rick says, "do you think the FBI should be alerted?" Tom shakes his head, and says, "I don't think it would be a good idea to notify them, because we don't want anyone to know about Johnny, and the less people that know about Robert Stevens being involved, is a big advantage to us."

The kids decide on the way to the hospital not to tell their dad about the twins going to the White House. They know their dad would put the kibosh on their plan, to plant surveillance bugs, in Robert Steven's office. When they arrive at the hospital, the kids all give their dad hugs, and Amie gives him the home made card she and Jimmy had made. They talk for quite awhile, then they say their good byes, and head for home.

On the way home Rick warns the twins, "if I allow you to go ahead with our plan to plant the bugs in the White House, you better be real careful. If anyone catches you, we will all be in serious trouble." Amie says, "noooo-way dude, dad would not let anything happen to us." Amie and Jimmy look at each other, as only twins can do. They know they are both thinking, about the exciting adventure that lies ahead.

They finally arrive home, and Amie calls out for Johnny. He is still keeping a low profile, because of the incident next door. He doesn't dare go near the windows, because Mrs. Dubay might see him, and put two and two together.

Johnny flies downstairs to greet his friends. Amie says, " dad is so proud of you for finding out about Robert Stevens, and says you are a valuable asset to us, for solving crimes." Johnny is beaming, as Amie is hugging him, and telling him, "you are such a good boy, I wish their were some way to contact your master, and tell him how much we enjoy having you live with us."

Johnny is hoping, if they ever find out about him messing up Mrs. Dubay's house, they will remember their dad's words, about him being a valuable asset.

Jimmy says, "would you like to go get some ice cream for being such a good boy." Johnny says, "would you go get the ice cream, I don't want to go outside for awhile." The twins are getting suspicious, and wonder why Johnny doesn't want to go outside. Jimmy says, "all right what's going on, why don't you want to go outside?. You might as well tell us what you have been up to, we will find out one way or the other, and you will be in more trouble, then if you tell us right now." Johnny confesses about the mess, he and Jake the dog made at Mrs. Dubay's house. They both roar with laughter, then try not to laugh. Amie says, "that was not very nice, and do not do anything like that again." Johnny tells them all about the red wine and the strawberry ice cream all over the white carpet. They both try to visualize the scene without laughing.

Finally, the day has come for their field trip to the White House. Rick drives the twins to their school in Roseville, and is lecturing them about being real careful not to get caught, and he asked "did you put the cell phone in your purse, in case you need to call me." She replies sarcastically, "yes Rick, honestly you are worse then Mrs. Bellinger, quit worrying." Jimmy gets involved, and says, "chill out Rick; everything is going to be fine." Rick replies a little nervously, "okay you two spies I'll see you later," and waves good-bye.

After their arrival, they see the Whiz and go running over to him. They also see some of their other friends, say their hellos, and give each other Hi-Five's.

They all get on the bus, as Jimmy says, "lets sit at the back of the bus where we can talk without the chaperones hearing." "Good idea," the Whiz says, and the three of them push their way through the crowd of kids to get the seats at the back of the bus.

Jimmy starts telling the Whiz, about Johnny, reading the mind of the President's Press Secretary, Robert Stevens, and their plan to plant surveillance bugs in the Press Secretary's office. Amie carefully pulls the bugs out of her bag, and says, "we each will be responsible for planting two bugs." She gives Jimmy and the Whiz their bugs, and keeps two for herself. Jimmy says, "we need to put them in his office and his briefcase, if we can find it. Also, the bathroom is a good place to put one in." The Whiz says, "good plan, I think it would be a good idea to stick one of the bugs under his desk, and the balance of the bugs, we'll stick anywhere in the office we can, without causing any suspicion." Amie pipes in to say, "the bugs are amazing, they'll stick onto any surface, and they pick up whatever is happening at that location. Rick will be at home listening to the bugs, and also, the bugs are being recorded, and when the time is right, we'll give the recordings to the FBI."

The Whiz says, "I always thought there was something weird about Mr. Stevens. I have only seen him on TV, but I always get bad vibes from him. Now we can find out, just how weird he is, and get him removed from the White House."

They are getting a little anxious about the bug planting, and their talking has subsided. Amie thinks, I have got to lighten up this situation as she begins to talk about Johnny, and telling the Whiz about Johnny's life and all the different trouble he has gotten into. Whiz says "he sure is something, and how is my bird friend doing?" Amie replies, "he's doing well, but we wish he could stay out of trouble." She goes on to tell the Whiz, about Johnny messing up Mrs. Dubay's house." The three of them start laughing uncontrollably. They are now feeling like happy carefree teenagers again. Whiz shakes his head and says, "WOW what a cool bird."

At last they arrive at the White House, as the bus driver parks the bus. The chaperones get off the bus first. They are standing in front of the bus door, and Mrs. Snider, who is a strict math teacher at school, instructs all of the kids to file off the bus in an orderly fashion, and stand together in-groups of five. Each chaperone will be responsible for one group. Whiz whispers to the twins, "I hope we don't get Mrs. Snider for our chaperone, she has eyes like a hawk, and ears like an elephant." They all giggle after that remark from Whiz.

Finally, all of the groups are assembled, and they are ready to enter the White House. The tour director has introduced herself as Miss Bridgett. She doesn't look much older than the students. Jimmy is thinking, I sure would like to know her better. Amie sees the admiring look that Jimmy is giving Miss Bridgett, and nudges him and says, "we are here to get a job done, and you better pay attention to business."

Miss Bridgett begins the tour by pointing to the beautiful grounds. As they are walking toward the White House, she is telling the group, "back in the mid 1800's a raging fire completely destroyed the White House. The White House was later completely rebuilt, but luckily none of the beautiful trees were affected, and many of the original ones are still living. If any on you would like to take pictures of the grounds now is a good time." The grounds of the White House truly are spectacular and many of the kids are snapping pictures. The landscapers work full time keeping the grounds looking perfect. Miss Bridgett mentions, "many famous White House functions have occurred on these White House lawns."

They climb the steps to enter the White House, and Miss Bridgett is talking nonstop, doing her best to pass on all of the knowledge she has about the White House. Whiz mumbles to Jimmy, "this is going to be one long tour, we are never going to get to the President's Press Secretary's office at this speed." Amie hears this and scolds them again to, "pay attention."

Miss Bridgett announces to the group, "we'll start with the kitchen." They all find a place to stand, while observing the kitchen chefs prepare a dinner for a foreign diplomat, and his wife. The kitchen is filled with the most wonderful aroma of food. They are introduced to the chef, who is a big jolly man, and takes time out to talk with the kids. He also prepared for them a huge plate of chocolate chip cookies and milk.

After the cookies are devoured, Miss Bridgett takes them from room to room, describing in detail, what each room represents. She also names endlessly, some of the famous people who have visited the White House, and is armed with many interesting facts, about some of the important decisions, that have been made for our country.

Finally they are in the Executive West Wing, where the Press Secretary's office is located. Now it is time for the teens to start their task of bug planting. They know this will have to be accomplished without anyone seeing what they are up to. Jimmy and Amie start asking Miss Bridgett an array of questions, causing the focus of attention to be on them. This clears the way for the Whiz to back out of the group without being noticed. Even Mrs. Snider who is listening intently to Miss Bridgett's speech doesn't notice that the Whiz has wandered to the back of the group near Robert Stevens desk, to stick one of the bugs under his chair.

The Whiz takes a deep breath, and looks back at Amie, who nods to him the coast is clear. As he makes his way to the back of the room, and bends over in pretense of picking up a pen, and presto, the second bug is placed under the desk.

Number one and two were a cinch. The Whiz tells Jimmy, "give me one of your bugs; I need it to place one by the telephone." He moves closer to the other side of the desk. As luck would have it, Mrs. Snider sees where the Whiz is, and motions for him to get back with the group. The Whiz waves to her, and says to himself whew, that was close as he makes his way back to his friends, and gives Jimmy back his bug.

Now it is time for Jimmy to place his bugs. He is somehow is supposed to get one in Robert Stevens bathroom, and one on the back wall. He places bug number three behind a picture near the bathroom. That was an easy one to get rid of.

The bathroom bug is going to be harder to get rid of. A light comes on in his head as he walks up to Mrs. Snider holding his stomach, and tells her, "I feel like I'm going to get sick, and need to use a bathroom right away." She hurriedly tells Miss Bridgett "I have a sick teen who needs to use a bathroom." Miss Bridgett makes the decision after looking at Jimmy, and says, "use the bathroom right over there, before you throw up all over everybody. What a mess that would be." Jimmy rushes in and starts making disgusting sounds like he is throwing up. He places bug number four behind the toilet tank. He goes back to his group, and says; "I'm feeling much better." Mrs. Snider asks, "are you sure, you sounded pretty sick." Jimmy answers, "yes Mrs. Snider, I'm feeling fine," as he stands near Amie and Whiz.

Mrs. Snider looks at him a little suspiciously, and thinks to herself without fail, there is always one student who gets sick.

They are only going to be in this office a few more minutes, and they still have two more bugs to go. Now it is Amie's turn to go into action. Her bugs are to be placed near the front door of the office, and the front sidewall. She decides to place them as the group is walking out of the office. She walks close to the sidewall, and sticks bug number five behind a picture. She lingers behind, so she can be the last one to walk out of the office, and puts the final bug on the inside of the door.

The three of them have a hard time keeping their composure, through the rest of the tour. They keep looking at each other feeling proud, their mission was successfully accomplished. They know this cannot be talked about, until they get home.

As they all get on the bus, the trio goes all the way to the back, and are high fiving and laughing at what they have just done.

On the trip back to Roseville, Amie calls Rick from their cell phone, to find out if the bugs are working. Rick says "I could hear you loud and clear. The bugs seem to be real powerful, and I don't think we need to plant that many bugs at one time." Amie says, "now we know, we won't have to buy as many next time."

Rick asks Amie, "how did your trip go, and what time do you want me to pick you up. Johnny is driving me crazy, asking real loud, where's Amie, where's Jimmy, when are we going to the zoo, I want to see Barbie. He has said that, at least a hundred times." Amie says, "Rick you are exaggerating but I know what you mean. Tell Johnny to calm down, and we will go to the zoo tomorrow, if that is OK with you."

The kids arrive back at their school. The twins and Whiz hug each other, and say their good byes. Rick honks his horn, as the twins spot his Mustang, and go running over to him. The relief was obvious on Rick's face, when he sees his siblings. The twin's adrenaline is still racing. Amie is practically yelling to Rick, "WOW was this an exciting day or what." Rick says to them, "it may have been exciting for you guys, but I was worried sick about something going wrong, and did you remember to wipe your fingerprints off the bugs?" Jimmy and Amie look at each other. Jimmy answers, "WHOOPS in our excitement we didn't think about that." Rick says sarcastically, "I sure hope your fingerprints aren't on file, or I will be visiting you two behind bars, if the bugs are spotted." Jimmy exclaims, "our fingerprints are on file, because dad had us fingerprinted when we were born, in case someone ever abducted us. "Don't worry, because dad would bail us out," Amie said. "The three of you did a great job, says Rick. "If dad only knew what you accomplished, he would be real proud of you. Unfortunately we are not going to tell him. We would be grounded for the rest of our lives." The twins still giggling agree with him.

On the ride home, Rick says the bugs are working great. The technology today is amazing. The recorder is set, and from here on in we'll be able to record, and hear everything that is going on in that office."

When they get home, Johnny comes flying downstairs, and squawks to them, "I wanted to go to the White House with you." Amie says, "parrots are not allowed in the White House, but we have a big surprise for you tomorrow."

Johnny's voice is now getting louder as he flies around the room, asking, "what's my surprise?" "Tomorrow is the day we go see Barbie," Amie tells him. Johnny says, "I sure hope she remembers me," Amie replies, "of course she does, you are so handsome she probably is in love with you." Johnny says, "I'm going to bed now so tomorrow will come faster." Everybody laughs as Johnny scurries off to bed.

The kids sit down to a delicious boiled dinner prepared by Mrs. Bellinger. Jimmy asks, "where's mom?" Rick says, "she called just before I left to get you kids, and said she was going to have dinner at a nice restaurant with Art Shaw." "Who is he," Amie asked in a curious voice. Rick says, "all I know is he also works for the FBI." Amie says "let's ask mom to bring him home to supper some time, so we can have Johnny check him out."

The next morning after breakfast, the trio and Johnny head for the zoo. When they arrive the twins tell Rick they are going to look around. Rick says, "I will take Johnny to the bird sanctuary," and then he says to Johnny; "you can't go in the birdcage this time. You will have to visit Barbie from outside the cage." Johnny says "OK boss but it won't be as much fun." Rick says, "I have to go to the zoo office for a few minutes, and you stay put." Rick goes to the office to talk to the zoo manager about buying Barbie. The zoo manager says, "she is not a rare bird, and you can have her for five hundred dollars." Rick says, " WOW" as he is writing the man a check. "You sure are going to make our parrot, and the twins very happy. Thank you very much." The zoo manager tells one of the zoo attendants to take Rick back to the bird sanctuary and get Barbie for him.

As they go back to the large birdcage. Rick spots Johnny sitting on the cage, with Barbie perched on the other side. There is a large crowd standing around the cage staring at the two parrots. One lady in the crowd remarks, "what a shame those two lovebirds can't be together." Immediately after she said that, the zookeeper approaches, and opens the cage door, and goes in to get the bird, and puts a tether on her, and brings her out to Rick. Rick puts Johnny on one shoulder and Barbie on the other, as the crowd cheers. Johnny asks, "where are we going with Barbie?" Rick replies, "she belongs to us now." Johnny is flapping his wings, jumping up and down with joy, and squawking "WOW- WOW." Rick laughs, and says, "let's go find the twins." Johnny says, "let me go find them, I can find them faster," as he flies off singing an old song called Barbara Ann-Barbara Ann, and within minutes, Johnny locates the twins. Johnny tells the twins, "Rick wants you to come right away, he has a surprise for you." The two kids go to look for Rick, with Johnny leading the way. As they get within eyeshot, they see Barbie sitting on Rick's shoulder, as they run the last thirty yards. When they get to Rick, Amie asks, "what are you doing with Barbie?" Rick replies with a big grin, "I just bought her." The twins both yell in unison, "you are the best brother in the world."

It was quite a sight seeing Johnny and Barbie sitting on Rick's shoulder's as they head for the car. They decide they had better put the top up on the Mustang, because they don't want to scare Barbie.

Rick says to Johnny "we have to purchase a bigger cage for the two of you. For tonight, you will have to make do with what we have, and we'll go shopping tomorrow for everything we need."

Rick explains to Johnny, "it will be your job to prepare Barbie to live with a human family. She has always lived with other birds, so she has a lot to learn. One thing for sure when it is bedtime, she will have to be taught to quiet down. We want this transition to be as smooth as possible for her, but we also have to consider our mother and Mrs. Bellinger. They will expect certain things of her, for instance, not flying right up to their faces, and scaring the wits out of them. Until she learns a few house rules, I think it would be a good idea for her to stay upstairs." Johnny is paying attention to Rick's instructions, and with a hearty squawk, he says, "Barbie will be good. Barbie is a smart girl, and with my help she will learn all the rules real fast." Rick thinks to himself about some of the trouble that Johnny has gotten into, now we are going to have double trouble. Oh well life will be twice as interesting as he looks at Johnny and Barbie.

Rick stops at the Seven Eleven to get some Big Gulps, for the three of them, and some ice cream for the parrots. Rick pulls in and parks the car next to this sleazy looking guy. Johnny is perched on the dash and gets a look at the man's eyes. Johnny thinks this is not good, that man is planning to rob the store. Johnny starts squawking to Jimmy, "to roll the car window up." Jimmy says, "okay Johnny the window is up, now are you happy." Johnny says to Jimmy, "we got big trouble I asked you to put the window up because, I didn't want the man in the next car, to hear what I have to say. I just read his mind, and he is going to rob this store." Jimmy knows the FBI has been following them, and they are parked a couple of cars away. Jimmy gets out of the car to warn the agents of the man's intentions.

The agent asks, "how can you be so sure the store is going to be robbed?" Jimmy replies excitedly "I overheard the man talking on his cell phone, telling someone that he is going to rob a store." Jimmy didn't dare, tell the FBI that Johnny read the bad man's mind. He knew that he wouldn't be believed, besides for Johnny's safety, the fewer people know the safer he will be. The older FBI agent says to Jimmy, "get back into your car and we'll handle this." Jimmy runs back and meets Rick in the parking lot. He tells him, "we have to get out of here now, the guy next to us is going to rob the store. I just informed the FBI, and they want us to get out of here, and wait down the street." Rick drives slowly out of the parking lot so as not to raise the man's suspicion. The bad guy does not see the two FBI men, parked at the end of the parking lot. He pulls out his gun as he goes in the store, and says, "this is a stickup." The two FBI agents go running to the front of the store. As they open the door and order the man to drop his gun, they shout, "we are FBI agents. Drop your gun." The man ducks down behind the counter, and starts shooting, and hits both agents, then runs out of the store. The kids hear the gunshots, and see the bad guy get in his car and race off. Amie is screaming, as Rick tells Jimmy, " go in the store to see if you can help, and I will follow his car." As the two of them race off after the bad guy, Rick says dial 911 and let them know what is going on." The bad guy's car is about six blocks ahead. Amie says, "hurry we don't want to lose him." "He can't out run my Mustang, and we can stay close to him," as Rick speeds up to eighty miles an hour, and gets within a half a block of the bad guy's car. Amie says "let's run him off the road." Rick says "we will leave that for the police."

Jimmy is back in the Seven Eleven. Both of the FBI agents are on the floor, and bleeding, but Jimmy says, "thank god you are both conscious." He asks the clerk, "did you call the police." The clerk says, "I did," and within minutes the store was surrounded by police cars, and the ambulance has also arrived.

Jimmy tells one of the policeman, "my brother Rick is following the robber, and gives them Rick's cell phone number." The patrolman immediately contacts Rick and asks him his location. Rick reports, "we are on interstate 295 going north, the last mile marker was 72, and we are going about ninety miles an hour." The officer says, "slow down, I don't want you injured, or anyone else on the freeway. We have your location, and are sending a couple of squad cars to catch up to you as we speak."

While the police are getting information from Rick, one of the other policeman is getting a description from Jimmy, of Rick's car and the robber's car. Jimmy gives them a complete description of both cars.

Rick is not about to slow down, despite the policemen's warning. Johnny and Barbie are perched in the back window, what a sight the two of them are, squawking and flapping their wings yelling, "bad man-- bad man don't lose the bad man." Amie is a little scared but knows Rick is a skilled driver. Never the less she checks her seat belt to be sure it is secure.

Rick floors the Mustang, and is now really speeding. Amie looks over at the speedometer, it is now over 100 miles an hour. The robber is cutting in out of traffic and passing everyone in sight. Rick is right behind him honking, and flashing his lights, and trying to warn the other cars to get out of the way of the danger.

In Rick's rearview mirror he can see the flashing lights of the approaching police cars. One of the policemen tells Rick through a speaker system built into the car for him to back off. Rick gets off the freeway at the next exit. Amie takes a deep breath; her heart is beating so hard she thinks it will jump out of her chest. "That ride, was more exciting than anything I have ever ridden at the amusement park." The parrots squawk, "fun ride lets do that again." The police have caught up to the bad guy, and try to get him to pull over, as he is thinking, where in the world did those cops come from so fast, as he goes faster.

The police have also been placed at the next few exits, on both sides of the freeway, making it impossible for the robber to flee for long. The robber is getting more careless with his driving, taking hazardous chances, and causing complete havoc on the freeway. For the safety of everyone, all entrances on the highway have been closed. The policemen's sirens are deafening, and the heavy traffic is doing their best to get to the side of the road, so the police have clear sailing.

The thief yanks his car out of his lane to pass another car, and catches the bumper causing him, and the other car to lose control. The innocent driver ends up in the southbound lane of the on-coming traffic. Luckily the cars see him coming and get out of the way in time. The cars in the other lanes missed the car only by inches. The bad guy's car goes out of control, rolls over several times before coming to a stop. The police are there immediately, and pull the man from his burning car, and can see he is not seriously injured. They get as far away from the burning car as fast as they can. They cuff him and wait for the ambulance, and the fire department.

Rick and Amie go back to the Seven Eleven. Jimmy runs out to meet them, and says, "the injured FBI men have already been taken to the hospital, and should be OK in a few weeks, and what happened to the scum that caused this?" Rick says, "I don't know we had to get off the freeway." The police commander walks over to the kids and says, "the crook has crashed his car, and has been captured, and isn't hurt too bad. He will be able to go to trial. Thanks to you kids; we have gotten a harden criminal off the streets. All of your names are going to be submitted to the nomination committee for your bravery." Rick says, "we appreciate that, but we feel it is our job to help when we can, and our dad is Thomas Winters a FBI agent." The commander says, "so you are related to that Thomas Winters, I know him very well. That explains where you kids get your bravery. I hear he is coming along very well, and that's great, he's a good man, and everyone is working very hard to find out who ran him over."

The commander shakes Rick's hand, and starts to walk away, then turns back and says, "by the way, we never located the cell phone of the robber." Rick replies "that's a real puzzler, he must have thrown it out the window during the car chase." The commander says, "sure, sure, that's probably what happened."

Johnny and Barbie are getting impatient for the kids to get back in the car. Johnny turns the radio on, and the two of them start singing. The customers that came to see what is going on, walking by Rick's Mustang, are being very amused at the two parrots singing along with the radio. The more people that look at the duet, the louder they sing.

When the kids go back to the car there is a group of people standing around. Rick says, "now what is going on?" They hear the parrots singing along with the blaring radio, that's playing an old Chuck Barry song, Johnny Be Good. The crowd is clapping and cheering encouraging the duo to continue. When the kids get into the car, Johnny and Barbie take a bow. As Rick is pulling out of the parking lot, Johnny yells out the window, "see you later alligator" and they all laugh.

When they arrive home, their mother and Mrs. Bellinger greets them at the door. Their mouths nearly drop open, when they see the kids bringing in two parrots. Rick says, "mom I know I should have checked with you first, but Johnny met Barbie at the zoo awhile ago. They fell in love and it seemed cruel to keep them apart." Amie chimes in, "Johnny will need company, when we are back in school." Mrs. Winters looks at the adorable couple, and says, "how can I say no. What's one more mouth to feed." Johnny asks, "speaking of food what's for dinner?" They all laugh and the kids say, "thank you mom, you won't be sorry." Mrs. Winters and Mrs. Bellinger look at each other shaking their heads

Mrs. Bellinger puts dinner on the table while the kids are chatting non-stop about Rick buying Barbie. Rick says nonchalantly, "oh by the way Barbie isn't the only thing that's happened today." Mrs. Winters asked with concern, "what else happened today? I don't know if I can take anymore surprises." Rick explains about Johnny alerting them, the Seven Eleven was going to be robbed, by a man sitting in the car next to them. He also tells her, "he wounded two FBI agents. The robber was caught by the police, and hauled off to jail." Rick deliberately leaves off the part about chasing the criminal, at high speeds down the freeway.

Mrs. Winters asks, "how are the FBI agents doing? Were they seriously hurt?" "They are going to be fine Jimmy answers." Mrs. Bellinger looks at Johnny and makes the comment, "since he has come to live with us, the children's lives, has been one adventure after another, and now that we have two parrots, life should be really interesting."

Amie says, "it's funny you should mention that. You wouldn't believe how well, the two of them sing together." Jimmy is talking with his mouth full saying, "after dinner we'll have them sing for you." Mom replies, "if they are as good as you say they are, we should enter them in the annual pet talent show." Amie asks, "is that the one we went to last year at the park?" "That's the one, I remember how much fun we had, watching all of the animals perform." Amie says, "let's do that, Johnny and Barbie can win hands down."

After dinner they bring the parrots downstairs, and Amie turns on the radio, and the birds start singing along. Mrs. Winters and Mrs. Bellinger listen intently with a surprise look on their faces. Mrs. Winters tells Mrs. Bellinger "that is absolutely beautiful. They sound just like the Everly Brothers singing Dream Dream Dream. First thing tomorrow we'll enter them in the contest." Jimmy, say's to Amie, "we can back them up, you play the keyboard, and I will play my saxophone." "Great let's find a song we all like and start practicing." Mrs. Winters says, "why don't you have them sing a patriotic song, like God Bless the USA, by Lee Greenwood. We have a tape of that song in the den." Jimmy tells everybody, "I love that song, and I will go get it, and see if the parrots can sing it."

Mrs. Winters asks Amie, have you talked to your father? She answers, "an FBI agent gave us a cell phone that cannot be traced. Dad has one too, so we can talk to him as much as we want He told us yesterday, he could come home in about three weeks. About the same time our house will be finished. He will still need physical therapy, and won't be able to work for several months. It sure would be nice if you would come back home and live with us." Mrs. Winters says, "the last week of the month, just before school starts, we are having a large teacher's convention in Las Vegas, for four days and I will be going, then maybe after that I'll come back home and help with your Dad's care." Amie says, "it would be wonderful to have you back."

They all settle down to watch TV. Rick is on the computer finding out about large birdcages for the two parrots.

The next day Rick and Jimmy drive to the pet store. They find the cage Rick had seen online, and purchase the cage. Rick puts the top down on his convertible, and they both tie the large box on to his car, and drive home. When they get home, Rick and Jimmy put the large cage together, in Amie's room. Johnny and Barbie are patiently waiting for them to finish. Johnny tells Barbie this is where we will sleep, and stay when nobody is home. Johnny walks into the cage with Barbie following, as he is singing, " Home-Home on the Range." The kids laugh, and leave the two parrots to themselves.

Johnny and Barbie spend most of their time singing, playing in the backyard, and walking around the neighborhood making friends. The neighbors love to be entertained by the two of them.

This Saturday is the pet amateur competition at the park. All of the proceeds are going to be given to the local animal shelter. The twins and the two parrots have been practicing, and sounding pretty good.

Saturday after breakfast the family gets into their mother's car, except Rick. He drives his own car, so he can take the two parrots and the kids musical instruments. They arrive at the park, and Amie goes to pick up their entry number for the contest, and they are given number twenty-five.

There are several good dog acts, and another parrot, that is pushing a monkey around in a baby stroller. That is pretty funny. They all laugh, and the crowd cheers. Finally it is their turn, to take to the stage. Jimmy grabs his saxophone, and Amie gets her keyboard, as Rick plugs in the amplifiers. The twins start-playing God Bless the U.S.A., as the crowd cheers them on. When Johnny and Barbie walk onto the stage and start to sing, you can hear a pin drop, the audience is astonished at the music coming out of the two parrots mouths. When they ended their performance the crowd goes crazy. They stand up, clap and shout, "ENCORE, ENCORE." Of course they steal the show, and get several standing ovations. Johnny says, "thank you very much ladies and gentlemen" (sounds just like Elvis, when he says that). The parrots march off the stage, bowing like a couple of hams. The emcee gets back on the stage, and the crowd starts yelling, "Johnny--Barbie" and the emcee tells the audience, "Johnny and Barbie have left the building." The crowd roars with laughter. They easily win the talent show, and are presented with the trophy. All of the acts take a final bow, while everyone applauds.

When the family returns home, Mrs. Winters, tells Mrs. Bellinger, "what a performance the parrots put on at the park. They got standing ovations and won the contest for their singing. Before they left the park, they got a couple invitations for singing performances at different children hospitals. They will call when they work out the details. The twins and the parrots need to work on some more songs they can sing together. It will probably be a little noisy around here for a little while."

Rick checks the tape recorder, and finally hears some incriminating conversations between Robert Stevens, and a man named Harold Hepler. They were talking about the November election, saying the President has too big of a lead in the polls, and they will need to do something to stop him. Rick tells the twins, "I need to get to work to find out who the man is that's responsible for running down our dad."

Amie says to Rick, "we have a date next week to entertain the children at St. Jude Children's hospital in Memphis, Tennessee. They are going to fly the whole family down there, and we need to practice some new songs to perform, that the kids will like."

Jimmy says, "I have an idea that should be cute," and asks Amie, "can you make, or have somebody make some puppet costumes, one of a hound dog and a teddy bear. Also an Elvis costume for Johnny, and a dress costume for Barbie. We need some small musical instruments. A saxophone, a small keyboard and a guitar for Johnny." Amie says "YA we will practice some Elvis songs, Elvis lived in Memphis. The kids at St. Jude should really enjoy Johnny's Elvis impersonator act. I remember reading about Elvis, he was known as the King of Rock 'n' Roll." Jimmy says, "that's a great idea, this is going to be a big hit."

The kids and the parrots work all week on five songs they think the children at St. Jude will like. Amie goes to a doll shop, to get the material to make what they will need for the show. Jimmy made a small guitar for Johnny, and the week goes by fast, as they stay busy getting ready for their trip.

The day arrives as a long white limousine picks the family up and drives them to the airport. Johnny is in one cage, and they had to buy another cage for Barbie. On the way to the airport the twins are real excited about the trip, as they have never ridden in a limousine before. Johnny asks quite loud, "is this what it is like to be a rock star?" Rick answers, "cool it dude you are not a rock star, you are just a parrot." Barbie cuts in and says, "ROCK-STAR, ROCK- STAR. My boy friend Johnny is a rock star." They all laugh as they reach the airport.

They meet the manager in the airport that organized the show, and he passes out their airline tickets. As they get near the check in point, Rick tells the parrots to, "keep quiet, or they won't let you on the plane." They both say at the same time "OK BOSS."

They all get settled on the plane, as Rick requested the parrots have their own seats. One with Jimmy, and one with Amie. Johnny says, "this is much better then flying somewhere by myself." They are in the air, and on their way to Memphis. The stewardess serves everyone juice and rolls, and asks Amie, where are you going with your parrots?" Amie replies with a proud smile, "we are going to entertain the kids at St. Jude." The stewardess asks," what tricks do your parrots do?" Amie says, "they sing and Johnny does impersonations." The lady says, "I have never heard parrots sing before, are they any good." Amie replies, "YA very good."

The stewardess says, "I would like to hear them sing," as she picks up the microphone, and tells the passengers about, "Barbie and Johnny the parrots who are going to St. Jude to sing for the kids." The passengers all agree they would like to hear them sing. The twin's take the parrots out of their cages, and Amie tells them "sing the same song they sang at the park, God Bless The USA." They sounded an awful lot like Lee Greenwood singing, and the song just blew everyone away. The passengers cheer and clap for over ten minutes. The stewardess came by, "you weren't kidding, they are great, the children at St. Jude will love them."

The flight is about three hours, and the time goes by fast. The passengers are now entertaining the parrots. Everyone who walks by stops to talk to them. One passenger in particular has a little girl with her who is going to be admitted to St. Jude for tests. The little girl's name is Sandy, a cute little tike with blonde curly hair. The mom tells them, "I can't thank you enough for singing that song. Sandy was so scared about having to go to the hospital, but listening to the parrots sing took her mind off being sick. Barbie says to the little girl, "I love your hair." Sandy beams as she asks Barbie, "can I touch your feathers?" Barbie answers her, "sweetie I would be honored." There was hardly a dry eye on the plane; everyone on the plane was touched. Mrs. Winters remarks, "this is exactly what we hope to accomplish, bringing joy to the children."

Before they know it, the stewardess is announcing, everyone fasten their seat belts please, we are getting ready to make our landing." The parrots are placed back in their cages and are ready for Memphis, Tennessee.

They leave the plane and are shuttled to the baggage area. It is an amusing sight, with the parrots in their cages and everyone stopping to take a second look at them. Of course Johnny can't resist his chance to be a comedian. He start's squawking, "let me out of this cage right now, I don't need an airplane to fly." Rick, laughingly tells Johnny, "we are all done flying, and as soon as we get our luggage, we are going to find our limousine and go to our hotel." They retrieve all of their luggage and flag down a redcap to help them with everything. Rick tells him, "we are being picked up by a limousine," Johnny interrupts, "oh boy we get to ride in another limousine."

The redcap pushes the baggage cart to the limousine area, and the Winters family follows behind him. Amie spots a man carrying a sign Winters Family. Jimmy exclaims, "WOW are we important people or what," as he runs ahead to let the limousine driver know they are the Winters family. Of course the limousine, driver already figured that out by spotting the parrots. It's not every day he has parrots for passengers. He thinks to himself just when you think you have seen it all, something new appears, as he shakes his head.

They are all situated in the limousine; and the glass partition is put up between the driver and the Winters clan. Rick lets the parrots out of their cages so they can look out the window to do a little sight seeing. The windows in the limousine have darkened windows, no one can see in but the parrots can clearly see outside. Mrs. Winters is thinking it is so cute to see the two of them staring out the window enjoying the sights of Memphis. The peace and quiet is also enjoyable. She also starts gazing out the window, to see what Memphis has to offer. Her thoughts are interrupted with the squawking of Johnny, asking for something to drink.

Mrs. Winters opens the refrigerator door and passes out refreshments. Johnny spots a beer in the refrigerator and says, "I'll have a beer," as he gets the look from Mrs. Winters. He says, "I was only joking," as she pours water for the parrots and gives them some grapes for a snack. Rick tells the parrots, "the Limousine Company called ahead to find out what special foods to have for you guys. I told them grapes are your favorite snack." Barbie says, "these are the best grapes I have ever ate," Johnny squawks "dee-licious." Jimmy laughs, "we never know what is going to come out of that crazy mouth of yours."

At last they arrive at their hotel. Amie says, "look at this place it looks like a castle. Are you sure we have the right place?" The limousine driver says in his southerly drawl, "yes ma'am this is the place." Mrs. Winters who is a world traveler cannot believe the beauty of this hotel.

The grounds are filled with Jupiter trees and Southern Oaks, along with beautiful rose bushes. The entire air is filled with the aroma of flowers. Johnny asks, "did we die and go to heaven?" Again they are all laughing at Johnny's humor. Rick asks, "what would we do without Johnny's smart remarks?" Jimmy says, "life would be pretty dull."

Mrs. Winters walks up to the front desk to check in. The front office girl looks twice at the entourage that has entered the hotel lobby. She was about to inform Mrs. Winters that animals are not allowed, when the front desk manager moves her aside and extends his hand to welcome the group to his hotel. The manager finishes checking them in and calls for a bellhop to show them to their suite. The twins look at each other, and Amie whispers, "did you hear that, we are going to get a suite." They both smile as the bellhop leads the way.

The hotel suite is bigger then their house, five bedrooms, a bathroom in every bedroom, with a hot tub and a shower, with gold faucets in every bathroom. They are on the top floor with a screened in balcony that is just the perfect place to keep Johnny and Barbie. Jimmy whistle's and asks, "who is footing the bill for all of this." Rick informs him, "good-hearted people, who want to bring a little joy, into the lives of the very sick children, pay for this."

It is getting late into the afternoon, Mrs. Winters suggest they order room service. They go over the menu and order their dinner. After dinner Mrs. Winters talks about getting everything set-up tomorrow at the auditorium. It is starting to get dark outside, and they decide to go out on the huge balcony, that is facing the west, and watch the beautiful sunset, and all the lights, of the big city. They are talking to each other, all at the same time, about how exciting this experience has been so far, and they get to stay here one more night.

Saturday after lunch, another limousine picks them up to take them to St. Jude. When they arrive at the large hospital, two men greet them at the entrance with a baggage cart, to take the things they need for the show to the auditorium. The auditorium is very big, and it kind of scares the twins that they will be performing in front of so many people. The manager tells them, "there will be about two thousand kids and adults in here. A lot of the kids that can't get out of bed will watch the show on live circuit TV." For the show they set up the puppet booth, and stage that St. Jude, has provided for them. They get the costumes, and put them on Johnny and Barbie, as Johnny is really hamming it up with his Elvis costume.

Johnny is prancing around with his Elvis cape trailing behind him. Johnny asks, "where are the scarves? I want to fly out into the audience, and give them as gifts, just like Elvis did!" Barbie is looking at Johnny as if he really is Elvis. Of course Barbie looks like a showgirl to Johnny, her costume is an exquisite gown, with a lot of glittering rhinestones in matching colors sewn on. The costume is completed with a tiara on her head. The outfits were purchased at the doll store, and Mrs. Bellinger made the necessary adjustments needed for the show. Mrs. Winters comments to the parrots, "what a beautiful couple you are." They both beam as Johnny squawks, "we are ready to give a really big, and I mean a really big sh-ooow." Now he sounds like Ed Sullivan. Mrs. Winters asks Johnny, "is their no end to your talents?" Johnny beams and replies "no ma'amm."

Rick says to the twins, "the parrots are ready," as they all get behind the curtain and get into their places. They wait for the band to start playing Zippity Do Dah, Zippity Aye. The curtain rises and the Emcee says, "ladies and gentlemen please welcome the amazing Johnny and his girlfriend Barbie." It's performance time; the twins put the parrots on a high table on the stage, in front of the puppet booth. Jimmy places the small guitar around Johnny's neck. The Elvis costume that Johnny is wearing has fake arms sewed on, and Jimmy places the Elvis arms on the guitar. It looks like Johnny is actually playing the guitar. Johnny starts out by saying, "these first two songs are a tribute to Elvis Presley." Then Johnny says, "thank you very much ladies and gentleman," and he sounds like Elvis talking, the audience roars. The twins take their place in the puppet booth.

Rick puts in the tape of the back ground music, and as trained, the parrots start singing Teddy Bear, with the puppets playing their musical instruments. The kids start clapping as the song ends. Johnny and Barbie go right in to the next song, Hound Dog. The puppets are dancing around playing in tune with Barbie and Johnny. The kids of St. Jude are having a very good time watching the parrots sing, and Johnny hamming it up in his Elvis costume. Their third song is God Bless the USA. This is the parrot's favorite song, and the kids, and the grownups alike, join in the singing of this very popular song. After the next two songs end, Johnny and Barbie take their bows, as Amie and Jimmy come out of the puppet booth to take their bows also. The crowd is clapping very loud and cheering. The emcee comes on stage and tells the kids, and parrots to take another bow, and says, "is that, great or what. Ladies and gentlemen our next act is nonother then the famous group ALABAMA. By popular request, their first song will be one of their many-many number one songs titled; There Are Angels Amongst Us. They have sung this song here before, and drew great appreciation from everybody." Just as expected the audience is awed by their performance. They sing two more songs, Amazing Grace, and How Great Thou Are. Alabama finishes their songs with a standing ovation.

The next act to perform is a number one songwriter, and country singer from Nashville, by the name of Jeff Raymond, known as the Sultan. Jeff comes on stage and says, "this is a number one song, I wrote a few years back, recorded by Eddie Rabbit, You Don't Love Me Anymore." Jeff sings another song named; "All I Have To Do Is Dream." Jeff gives another outstanding performance and also, receives a standing ovation.

Jeff thanks the crowd and makes a short speech about how important our children are, and says, "what about those parrots. We are all here to show our support and love for the children of St. Jude's Hospital." He walks off the stage, waving to the appreciative audience. The emcee comes back on stage, "we have one more song, and we would like everyone to join in and sing. Those of you who are able please follow Alabama around the auditorium singing, when the Saints go Marching in." What a wonderful scene it is to observe the children, some of them in wheelchairs, and some of them walking with canes and crutches having the time of their lives, clapping and singing with the band. They forget for the moment, about all of the tests and treatments they have had to endure in their short little lives. Johnny and Barbie fly through the audience dropping scarves from their mouths to the delighted children. To soon the show is over with, and everyone takes a final bow.

After the concert every one is milling around, signing autographs, for all of the children, and eating the buffet they have set up for everybody. It is quite a sight, Johnny and Barbie sitting on the laps of the children in wheelchairs. The concert manager comes up to Mrs. Winters and Rick. "This was one of the greatest events we have ever had here. Your birds and twins are very talented, and we have more shows for them if that is OK." Mrs. Winters tells him, "school is starting in two weeks, and they will be very limited at what they can do. But next summer they will be able to take on a few." George the manager asks, "can we take the parrots, by themselves to entertain?" Mrs. Winters replies, "I doubt it, but I will discuss it with the family and let you know."

The party goes on for another hour, then they take the limousine back to the hotel.

Back at the hotel everyone is still going over the show, and they are all talking at once. Mrs. Winters says, "did you see the joy on the children's faces during the performance?" Amie says, "mom, it was priceless, worth more than a zillion dollars. I'll never forget this day ever, and tears well up in her eyes as she thinks about the children." Jimmy even looks a little teary eyed. Jimmy says, "maybe we can do this again." "We'll certainly try," says Mrs. Winters as she thinks to herself what a wonderful family I have.

The twins and Rick go to the hotel pool to enjoy it for the last time. Johnny and Barbie are pretty tired from all of the excitement, and retire to the balcony. Mrs. Winters and Mrs. Bellinger, enjoy the peace and quiet, as they watch TV and talk about the show.

The next day they have a quick breakfast and throw their belongings into their suitcases. It doesn't take them long to get ready for the return trip home. After the excitement from yesterday even the parrots are quiet. When they are completely packed they call for their limousine to take them to the airport.

They board the airplane for the three-hour journey home. After they have boarded, Rick recognizes two FBI agents sitting behind them. He walks back to talk to the agents. They have all been so busy with the show they have forgotten that the FBI are following them, to assure their safety. Rick asks them, "were you on the plane to Memphis with us?" The familiar looking agent answered, "we were not, but we had two other men watching you." Rick thanks them, shakes their hands and returns to his seat. They rest on the plane and arrive safely back in Washington.

They arrive home exhausted from the three days of fun they had. Rick checks their messages to hear their house is ready for them to move back into. Their Dad will also be coming home at the same time.

Monday morning the kids tell their mom good bye. They all pile, along with the two parrots into Rick's Mustang. It is a real nice day and Rick decides to put the top down on his convertible. They head for Roseville, as both parrots are squawking, "is this wonderful, or what."

When they get home, their dad is already there, along with two FBI agents, and one of them is the beautiful Christine Casey, dad's friend and FBI agent. Everybody hugs, and the kids say, "we are glad to have you home dad." Tom goes over to the two parrots, and rubs the top of Johnny's head and says, "I have been hearing a lot of wonderful things about you young man, and I would like to meet your girlfriend." Johnny says, "this is Barbie, and Barbie meet Tom Winters, the kids father." Barbie replies back, "you have a very nice family Mr. Winters." Mr. Winters says to Barbie, "you talk real good too, and I hear you two were a big hit at the St. Jude's hospital with your singing." Barbie says, "Ya and my boy friend sounds just like Elvis does on TV." Tom smiles at her and says, "that's great, glad to have you with us."

The kids take a tour of the house. They carry their luggage up to their bedrooms and Amie says, "everything looks great." Jimmy says, "it feels so good to be home. Let's call Whiz and let him know we are back." Amie says "I wonder if the Whiz is still grounded from our house." "After his kidnapping I don't think he'll ever be allowed over here again. You know parents, they think kidnapping is a big deal," Jimmy says and they both giggle.

Amie calls Whiz, and Jimmy gets on the extension phone. They tell him all about their Memphis trip and how they entertained the kids at St. Jude's Children's Hospital. Whiz says, "dang, I wish I could have been there." Amie says, "don't worry we have a video of all the performances. When you come over we'll watch it with you." Whiz says, "I'll ask my folks if I can come over, and I will let you know."

Rick goes to the third floor and sets up the recorder from the secret White House bugs. Dad doesn't know about the bugs and the recorder, Rick is afraid they will be in big trouble if dad knew about them. There is nothing new on the recorder except routine activities and appointments. Rick is disappointed, he was hoping by now that Mr. Stevens would have said something, or had someone in his office that would give him some clues to find out exactly what they are up to. Rick goes downstairs to join his dad and Ms. Casey.

Christine and Mr. Winters are deep in conversation, as she is updating him on what they have found out. She revealed to Tom, the name of the second guy on the boat was Jack Thorton. She says, "he was the one that jumped overboard, and we found his body." Tom asked, "what was the cause of death, drowning?" Christine answers and says, "surprisingly no, he was found with a bullet in his head." Rick walks in the room and hears everything Christine has said. Rick exclaims, "wow somebody wanted to shut him up for good." Mr. Winters comments, "this is a tough crowd we're dealing with son, they don't mess around if you get in their way." Rick says, that's for sure."

Christine continues talking, "we don't have all of the answers yet, but we believe the press secretary Robert Stevens is involved in some way." Rick wishes he could tell the two of them about the conversation he heard from the White House, but he knows, at this time it has to be kept a secret.

Rick excuses himself and decides to get on the computer and types in the name of Harry Hepler. This is another name he got from the White House roster. Nothing of interest comes up about him.

Rick starts planning his trip back to college. He says, "I am going to take courses on becoming a private eye." Dad says, "so you think becoming a private eye sounds exciting. If you are serious about this vocation, I know a couple of guys that have been real successful private detectives. When the time is right I will introduce you to them, perhaps they would give you some pointers."

Later, Jimmy, and Amie go outside to play with the parrots. They see a man get out of a car and walk toward them. All of a sudden Johnny starts squawking, "HUD, HUD" as he flies over to him. Hud says, "Johnny, I'm so relieved that you are okay, I thought I would never see you again." As he hugs Johnny he asked the kids, "how did you end up with Johnny?" They both fill him in about how they found Johnny beat up lying on the sidewalk. Johnny pipes in; "Mrs. Handly beat me up because I drank her last beer." Hud says, "she told me that you flew off because you missed me." Jimmy says, "we gave Mrs. Handly our phone number to give to you when you returned."

"When did you get home?" Johnny asked Hud. "I have been back for a couple of weeks, and have been searching everywhere for you. I even placed an ad in the local newspaper. I can't believe that you were just down the street from my apartment." Hud notices the other parrot and asked Johnny, "who is this cute little girl?" Johnny beams, "this is my girlfriend Barbie, I met her at the zoo." Jimmy says, "my brother Rick bought her to keep Johnny company when we all return to school in the fall." Hud says, "Johnny you were very lucky to find such a caring family."

Amie says to Hud, "we sure love him, but we know he belongs to you." Hud asks Johnny, "Would you like to remain here?" Johnny answers, "I sure don't want to leave the kids and Barbie." Hud replies, "you don't have to Johnny, it's not fair anyway, because I am gone so much, and besides, I just live down the street. After I talk to Mrs. Handly about how she treated you, I plan on moving. However, I'll look for a place close to here, so I can visit you." Johnny says, "I'll miss you, and all of our adventures together." Hud replies, "your not getting rid of me that easily, and I'll be checking up on you, and your girlfriend Barbie." Hud also volunteers to watch the two parrots, if the family needs to go out of town. Hud and the twin's exchange telephone numbers and addresses. Hud informs Johnny, "I'm going to have a talk with Mrs. Handly about how she treated you, and I imagine I won't be welcome there. I can stay at the motel down the street, until I can find a new apartment in this area."

The twins tell Hud all about some of the things they have been up to. Jimmy tells him about Johnny reading a man's mind at the beach, and the man getting arrested trying to break into their home. They also tell him about the fire, their friend Whiz getting kidnapped, and Johnny helping rescue him. The best time of their lives, was when they all went to Memphis, Tennessee to sing for the sick kids at St Jude children's hospital where Johnny and Barbie both became stars. Hud says, "WOW I knew that Johnny could sing a little bit, but he never knew the words to the songs he sang." Amie tells Hud, "Johnny watches a lot of TV, and that is how he learned the words to all the songs he knows. Also Johnny can do a great imitation of Elvis." Hud says, "It sounds like you have been busy Johnny, and I can't wait to hear you sing."

Amie invites Hud to come in the house to meet their dad. Hud at first declines, saying, "I don't want to interrupt your dad." Jimmy says, "my dad has been waiting to meet you, and besides we can't wait to tell him, that Johnny is ours forever." Hud says, "okay, if you are sure I won't be bothering him."

As they go into the Winters house, Amie is telling Hud about their mom and dad being separated. "We live with our dad, although we also spend a lot of time at mom's house too." Johnny squawks to Hud, "we all stayed with Mrs. Winters after the house fire, and she is a nice lady." Hud asked the twins, "what line of work are your parents in?" "Mom is a schoolteacher, and dad works for the FBI, and what kind of work do you do?" Hud says, "I work for the government also, and have you ever heard of N.C.I.S?" Jimmy says, "I sure have, that must be an important job." Hud says, "I also used to be a Navy Seal member." Jimmy says, "that's cool dude." The kids take Hud inside to meet their dad. Christine Casey is still there, although it looks like they are wrapping up their meeting. Jimmy introduces Hud to the both of them. You can tell Hud is instantly attracted to Christine. Hud is thinking to himself, I wonder where this beauty has been all my life. He shakes both of their hands, and thanks Tom for taking in Johnny. Hud says, "it looks like you saved Johnny's life." It was the twins that rescued

Johnny, I just agreed to let him live here, as if I had a choice, those kids love animals," Tom said.

Christine asks Hud, "what part of navel intelligence do you work for." "I have just been transferred to criminal activities for Iraq, but I will spend most of my time in Arlington, "Hud replied.

Hud tells them about his trip to Iraq and the men he put away for selling our guns to the bad guys. "Somehow they are tied to people, working in the White House. Christine says, "Wow, maybe the men we are investigating at the White House are connected. We will have to get together and compare the information we have." Hud asks "where is your office, I will come there tomorrow." Christine answers, "we have an office at the Pentagon." "I can be there by noon, don't eat, we can have lunch to discuss this further." Christine says "great." Tom senses some excitement in her voice, as he has, kind of liked her for sometime, but he still has feelings for his wife. The kids have not told their Dad about keeping Johnny yet. Tom says," are you going to take Johnny home with you?" "No" he says, "I can't do that to your family, and the two parrots. That is if you don't mind keeping him, but I would like to take Johnny with me once in a while." Tom says, "that would be great." Tom knows Hud will probably use Johnny for his mind reading abilities, but he can't say that out loud because Christine doesn't know about Johnny.

Hud has to leave because he wants to talk with Mrs. Handly while she is still sober. They all shake hands and

Johnny says, "hope I will see you soon." Hud replies, "you bet you will." Hud looks at Christine; "I will see you tomorrow for lunch." Christine smiles sweetly, "it's a date," she replies. The whole family agrees that Hud is a nice man. Amie is so happy now that they don't have to worry about giving Johnny back; she dances around the room with joy. Mr. Winters could tell that Johnny and Hud have a very strong bond, and knows that it was not an easy thing for Hud to do, giving up Johnny. Mr. Winters says, "Hud is an honorable man."

Jimmy walks Hud to the door, and Hud reminds Jimmy that it is, "very-very important too keep Johnny's gift a secret. Men would kill to have that much power." Hud waves and, again he says, "thank you."

Hud returns to his apartment house, and confronts Mrs. Handly about what she did to Johnny. He says, "Johnny, and the twins told me what happened, and what you did to him." She says, "I am really sorry, but he took my last beer." Hud laughs and says, "so that is what this was all about. Johnny will not be coming home, he is going to stay with the Winters family down the street, and Johnny has stopped drinking. That little episode scared the wits out of him, and because you apologized, I will stay in my apartment."

Back at the Winters house Tom says, "I have a surprise for you two," and hands them two cell phones, and says, "they are Ipod phones. They can take pictures, and can be tracked wherever you are." "Dad, thank you very much," Amie exclaims. Jimmy hugs his dad, "thank you, wait till we tell Whiz what we have."

Mrs. Winters has called to talk to Rick, "the people that organized the Memphis trip, wants the kids and the parrots to perform on Saturday, at the local cancer hospital for about two hundred kids." Rick says, "great", the twins and the parrots will be excited about performing again. I will see you Saturday, but hang on dad would like to talk to you." Rick walks over to his dad, hands him the telephone, "mom would like to talk to you." Grinning because neither one said anything, about talking to the other. Mr. and Mrs. Winters talk for a long time. Rick and the twins smile at each other and Amie says, "that's a good sign." All three kids have hopes their parents can get back together.

Tuesday the Whiz comes over. They watch the video that they had taken of the Memphis concert. The Whiz says, "you guys are really, very good together. I loved you two as puppets, and I never knew parrots could sound that good. I wish I could have been there." Amie says, "parrots are great imitators, we leave MTV on all of the time for them to listen to. We also put on the country channel, that way they can learn different types of songs."

Amie says, "I have a great idea, we are going to the cancer hospital in DC on Saturday to perform, why don't you bring your guitar and come with us? That is, if your parents aren't still mad." "They told me I could come over here today, and since your dad was back home, and the FBI are watching your house it would be OK." Amie says, "okay, we have a date, go home and get your guitar so we can practice." Whiz leaves singing to himself and yells out the back door "be back in a flash."

While the Whiz is gone, Amie calls Hud and asks, "can you come to the hospital on Saturday, to watch our performance?" "I'm very honored you thought to call and invite me. I wouldn't miss it for the world. Thank you, and I will see you Saturday."

Whiz returns with his guitar, as Amie calls Jimmy and asks, "can you come upstairs to help with the song selections?" The hospital spokesman has told them, they will need to perform five songs. After going through many songs, they finally make their choices. Johnny and Barbie are patiently waiting and singing, "There's No Business like Show Business." Whiz says, "I think the parrots are ready for rehearsal."

The rehearsals the rest of the week goes well, and everyone is feeling ready for the big show. Now they have two hams to put up with, Johnny and the Whiz, they are so comical trying to outdo each other. The Whiz no matter how hard he tries, cannot do an Elvis imitation. Johnny acting a little superior tells him, "keep practicing dude you will get it eventually," and then he and Barbie start snickering at the Whiz.

Saturday the whole family except Mr. Winters, and Mrs. Bellinger pile into the Winters van, and drive to pick up the Whiz. The Whiz walks out of his house with his guitar, playing an Elvis tune, "You ain't nothing but a hound dog." The family bursts out laughing, and Rick tells him, "you are a bigger ham than Johnny is."

They arrive at the hospital and meet Mrs. Winters and go directly to the cafeteria to set up for their performance. Mrs. Winters puts Barbie and Johnny on the table, where they will perform their act. The trio and the two parrots have memorized the five songs. Mrs. Winters asked, "what order are you going to sing your songs? Jimmy replies, "first we will sing Wooden Heart. The second song we have chosen is Brush Those Tears from Your Eyes. The third selection is Daddy's Girl. My favorite selection is fourth and is titled, There are Angels amongst us." Amie pipes up, "last but not least is my favorite, May the Good Lord Bless and Keep you." Mrs. Winters compliments the children on their song selections.

After the five songs are completed, they mingle with the children, and can see the delight on all their faces. Everyone at the concert keeps coming up and congratulates them and the parrots on their performance. Mrs. Winters smiles, "what a wonderful thing you children, and the parrots have done."

Hud rushes up to the group and says, "Bravo, Bravo," as he presents Barbie with a beautiful bouquet of red roses. "What a wonderful show, I enjoyed every minute of it. Johnny you rascal, keeping your talent such a secret. Johnny and Barbie your duets are unbelievable, and Johnny, you knew all of the words. And they say television isn't educational."

They all enjoy the dinner the hospital has put on for them. The room is filled with laughter, and the children, as sick as they are, are still wound up from the concert. Adding to the excitement, the parrots wander around talking to all the children, and the children enjoy watching them eat their grapes, and ice cream. Johnny squawks, "beer used to be my favorite treat, but now ice cream is and everyone laughs.

They talk for awhile, and Mrs. Winters says, "I hate to bring this party to an end so soon, but I have to get to bed early, for my early flight in the morning to Las Vegas. The annual teacher's conference starts on Monday." She reaches in her purse to give Rick the itinerary, in case they need to get a hold of her. Hud says, "I have to get going too, and Johnny I will see you again real soon." Johnny says, "bye boss."

On the ride home Whiz is still high from the excitement, of performing for a crowd. He tells the group, "I enjoy performing more than playing games on the computer." Jimmy and Johnny look at each other and Jimmy says, "I think we have created a monster." Whiz starts singing VIVA Las Vegas, and Johnny joins in, then everyone is singing including Mrs. Winters. They sing all the way to her house. The twins kiss their mom good bye, and tell her, "play some slots for us," she laughs and waves good-bye. Then the kids head for Roseville.

Lois Winters rather than driving through the crowded traffic, decides to call a taxi. She thinks to herself there is no sense getting stressed out over traffic, she grabs her morning paper, and the cabby takes her luggage. She sits back to enjoy the ride to the airport.

The airport is also crowded. However the lines move fast and before long, she is at a gate waiting to board the plane. She hears her seat number announced by the airline and finds her seat, and settles in for the long flight to Las Vegas.

Lois gets a window seat and a young looking girl sits next to her. As the huge plane takes off, the young girl asks, "how long is this flight suppose to take?" Lois replies, "the airline said about four and one half-hours." The girl says, "my name is Courtney." Lois extends her hand, and replies, "my name is Lois." Mrs. Winters asks, "what are you going to Vegas for, you look too young to gamble?" Courtney laughs, "I'm twenty four and a showgirl at the Wynn casino, and I live in Las Vegas. I was in DC for my grandmother's funeral, she was ninety-two." Lois says, "I'm really sorry." Courtney asks, "what is your trip about?" "I'm a schoolteacher, going to a teacher's convention, and I'm also staying at the Wynn." Courtney says, "great, maybe we can share a cab." Lois replies, "that would be great." After a lot of different conversations the plane lands. The two of them go to the baggage claim to get their bags. They get a cab outside the terminal, and they both comment on the way to the hotel, about how hot it is in Las Vegas. Mrs. Winters also comments about getting married in Las Vegas, twenty-five years ago, and how she really has feelings for this town. They say good-byes as Lois checks in, and the bellhop shows her to her beautiful room overlooking the Las Vegas strip.

After relaxing for awhile, Lois looks at her watch, as she is supposed to meet Art Shaw at three o'clock in the lounge for drinks. She hurries to the lounge, and Art is already there. He says, "I flew in from Dallas Texas, where I have been on assignment." They talk for awhile, and after three drinks, and three hours later Lois is getting a little tipsy, as she usually doesn't drink. Art has been questioning her about her husband's accident. She tells him what the kids told her they overheard their father tell Christine Casey, about some bad men at the White House. She thinks to herself his questions are odd, but he is a FBI agent. Art is thinking, this is not what I wanted to hear. Lois excuses herself to go to the restroom. After she gets up Art puts a heavy dose of sleep medication in her drink.

Lois comes back from the restroom, and then they go to her room, where she immediately passes out. Art ties her up, gags her, then goes out and buys a large trunk, and rents a van and drives back to the hotel. No one thinks it strange as the bellhop delivers the large suitcase to Lois Winters room. Art puts Lois in the suitcase, and calls the bellhop back to the room, the bellhop, of course not knowing the woman is inside, take's it down stairs and puts it in the van.

Art drives to North Las Vegas where he has rented a warehouse and meets another man and says, "watch the woman and do not let anything happen to her unless I call back with the code 888, then you are to dispose of her." Art knows eventually, he will have to do something with her. He thinks what a mess I have gotten myself into, when I accepted a large bribe from Robert Stevens. I never thought it would involve hurting my friends.

Amie tries to call her mother on Tuesday and leaves a message for her to call her back. When she doesn't hear from her, she calls again with no luck. Thursday she tries again, now she is really getting worried and tells her dad. Tom calls the Las Vegas FBI, and talks to an agent he knows, and asks him, "will you check to see where Lois is? " The Winters family is really worried when she doesn't arrive home on Friday's flight. The Las Vegas FBI agent Joe Kylman has kept Tom Winters up-dated on the search for his wife. Tom hears again from Joe late Friday night, and reports back, "I am sorry there is no trace of Lois, and I have discovered that your wife did not attend any of the scheduled meetings or luncheons provided by the conference. We went over the hotel videotapes, and they showed her going in and out of her room on Sunday, so we know she arrived in Las Vegas safely. But this is really peculiar, later that day the hotel tapes are blank, so unfortunately her where abouts can only be tracked until late afternoon." Unknown to the hotel security Art had broken into the surveillance tape room, late that night, and removed the late afternoon tapes.

Tom calls the kids together, to inform them of the situation with their mom. Amie, and Jimmy both are crying. Amie is sobbing to her dad, "I don't understand why this is happening. First you are nearly killed, by a hit and run driver, now mom is missing." Tom hugs the twins and says, "I survived my accident, and we will find your mom." Rick is upset, but he is trying not to show any emotions in front of the twins. He clears his throat and says, "dad is right we are going to find mom, I just know it." Mr. Winters is thinking that his job might, somehow be related to the fact that she is missing, and he is very worried.

After a restless night's sleep, Tom gets up and checks his e-mail. It is very alarming. The message tells him, if he ever wants to see his wife again, he had better back off the case about the White House. Tom mutters to himself, "why didn't I have protection for Lois too?" He calls Rick into his home office, and shows him the e-mail. They agree for the moment not to tell Joe, the FBI agent in Las Vegas.

Rick says, "I'm not the FBI, I can fly out to Vegas and nose around. After all I wouldn't raise any suspicion by whoever these people are. They'll think I'm just a kid looking for my mom, and I don't think they would look at me as a threat." Tom tells his son, "I do not want to put you any danger. We have enough problems, with the danger that I have placed your mom in." "Dad, nothing is going to happen to me," Tom says, "perhaps you are right, they wouldn't be threatened by you."

The next day Rick is on a plane flying to Las Vegas. He spends a couple days investigating, and talking to everybody in the hotel. He finally talks to a bartender, and shows him a picture of his mom, and the man thinks he waited on her. He tells Rick, "she was with a man, that I hadn't seen before." Rick doesn't know what to do now, so he heads back home.

After arriving home Rick asked his dad, if he could help get a pistol for him for protection. Tom answers thoughtfully, "that would be a good idea, but by law, you have to take a course on the shooting range. That will only take a couple days, and I can have a friend rush through the license, and I also want you and the twins, to take a self-defense class, and you can start right away." Rick says, "fine I will go tell the twins, and call and get us signed up."

That evening Rick calls Art Shaw. He asked him, "have you heard from my mother?" Art replies quickly, "no, but I would like to come over and talk to you." Rick replies, "fine, when are you coming?" "I can be there in an hour," Art tells him. "We'll see you then." Rick is thinking that's strange, how does he know where we live. Rick tells his dad about the conversation, and his dad agrees, " that is strange. Rick, have Johnny ready when Mr. Shaw gets here, and tell him to look and listen, to see if he can find out what is going on. Make sure Johnny doesn't say anything until he leaves."

When Art arrives he asks Rick and Tom, "do you have any idea why Lois was kidnapped?" They both agree that they have no idea. The conversation continues with Art, and he acts like he really cares, at the same time Johnny is sitting close to him, as Art is thinking about what he did to Lois. Art looks at Johnny, Rick asks him, "do you want to hear Johnny sing?" Art was definitely not interested in hearing Johnny sing, and he replies, "maybe another time, right now I have to go."

After he leaves Johnny squawks, "that man has our mom." Tom sits up straight in his chair, "now what in the world has he got to do with this case. We can't tell anybody about this because of the e-mail warning." Amie pipes in, "I think we can trust Hud, maybe he will help us." Tom tells Rick, "go over to his house we don't dare talk on the telephone." Rick says, "maybe we can use those secret phones, your FBI friend gave the twins, to talk to you while you were in the hospital." Tom answers, "no you had better go over there," Rick agrees. Rick walks the short distance to Hud's house. Hud is glad to see Rick, and asks, "what brings you here?" Rick tells him, "our mother has been kidnapped, and we received a threatening e-mail, and also tells him what Johnny found out about Art Shaw."

Hud tells Rick, "I really feel terrible about your mother, and I will help in any way I can." Rick tells him about the bartender in Las Vegas. Hud says, "I will get a picture of Art Shaw, and we can take it to Las Vegas, and have the bartender look at the photo." Rick tells Hud, "I am very grateful, but you can't tell anybody at

NCIS because my mother's life is in danger and we don't know who to trust." Hud replies, "there is one person I can trust my life with, and his name is Keith Gaines. I will have him do a background check on Art Shaw, and have him followed. I have some vacation time coming and I will use it to see what we can find out about your mother's kidnapping. I'll get a hold of the airlines and make arrangements for the two of us to catch a flight to Vegas first thing in the morning." Rick shakes his hand, and thanks him again, and says "see you in the morning."

The two of them catch a morning flight out of Washington DC. When they arrive in Las Vegas, it is still early because of the three-hour time difference. Hud rents a car, and they drive through heavy traffic to the Wynn hotel.

The bartender hasn't arrived yet so they have lunch, and wait for him to begin his shift. At twelve o'clock Vegas time the bartender comes on duty. Rick points him out and Hud and Rick approach him with the photo of Art Shaw. He remembers Rick, and tells him, "yes that is the man, that was with your mother."

They thank the bartender for his help, and Hud leaves him a twenty-dollar tip. Rick asks, "what now? They must have had some way of getting her out of here." Hud answers, "let's go question the bellhops to see if anyone might have seen her." Rick says, "good idea I didn't think of that when I was here before." They show the pictures to the bellmen, and the older bellhop says, "the man in the photo gave me twenty dollars to take a large trunk out to a van."

Okay Rick, "let's go back to the airport, and check with the rental car companies." When they get there Rick says, "wow there must be fifty rental car companies here." "We can narrow that number down in a hurry," Hud tells him. "The FBI and NCIS only have contracts with Avis and Alamo car rentals." Hud and Rick walk into the Avis Rental, and Hud hands his ID to the agent. He asks the attendant, "has anyone by the name of Art Shaw rented a car in the last week or so?" The clerk is scanning through the rental logs and replies, "Mr. Shaw rented a van last Sunday." Hud says, "now were getting somewhere." He asks the clerk, "has the van been returned?" The clerk replies, "no, it's not due back for a few days."

Hud tells Rick, "the best thing about rental car companies, all of their cars are equipped with GPS tracking devices. That's in case, if any of their cars come up missing, they'll know exactly where to find them." Rick tells the clerk, "I need to check the Global Tracking Company on the Avis computer." As they are walking to the computer room Hud explains to Rick, "the tracking device on the computer will tell us the exact location of the van."

They go through the records and discover that the van is parked in North Las Vegas. Rick writes the address down and Hud picks up a map from the Avis attendant.

Rick looks at the map, and sees that U.S 15 is the route they need to take. The traffic in Vegas is heavy and moving slow. Hud starts driving and says to Rick, "I know a shortcut that will get us out of this traffic." At last they are in North Las Vegas, and they spot the van. Hud says, "good let's park where we can see the van without being noticed." He sees a parking place across the street, pulls in and they begin their wait to see if anyone claims the van.

They sit for quite a while; finally a suspicious looking man comes out of a nearby warehouse and gets in a car and leaves. It is now dark. Hud walks up to the warehouse, to see if he can see in any of the windows, to no avail. He returns to the car, and they wait for another hour. Finally the same man comes back. As he is getting out of his car, Hud sneaks up from behind, and knocks the man unconscious. Rick comes over to where they are, and asks, "what now?" Hud gets the mans keys, and says, "I hope he is alone." They unlock the door and very quietly go inside. They walk down the long hall. Hud holds up his hand for Rick to stop. He points to the door and whispers, "there is another man inside and tells Rick to knock, when he comes out, run into the next room." When the man comes out Hud is standing behind the door, and hits him on the head with the end of his gun. Rick rushes into the room. His mother is sitting in the corner, tied-up and gagged. Rick quickly unties her, and removes her gag. She stands up with Rick's help. Mrs. Winters starts crying, and hugs Rick for a long time. She tells the two, "thank you very much, I thought I was a goner, they talked about getting rid of me." Rick tells his mother, "it was Hud that saved you, he is a very brilliant agent. Most people would never have thought to do what he did to find you." Hud says, "we had better get out of here. Let's drag this thug outside to their van." Hud puts both men in the van, and tells Rick, and Mrs. Winters, "drive the rental car back to the airport and hop a plane back to Washington. Meanwhile I'll turn these two in, if I can find somebody to trust. Then I will take the next available flight back." Rick says, "let me help tie them up before we leave." Mrs. Winters hugs Hud again and says "thank you very much, I know you saved my life." Hud shakes both their hands, and says; "I will see you both back in Washington."

They arrive at the rental car terminal and return the car, then take the shuttle bus back to the airport. They purchase a ticket for Mrs. Winters and wait for their flight. Rick calls the number of the secret phone of Amie's. When she answers, Rick tells the news, and then he puts his mother on the phone. The Winters household is going crazy with excitement, even the parrots are walking around singing, "mom's free--mom's free." Lois Winters tells, Amie, "calm down and put Jimmy on the phone." They talk for awhile, then Mrs. Winters tells him to meet them at the airport at seven thirty. She tells, Jimmy, "I love you very much, and I'll see you tonight, and give everybody a hug for me."

Tom calls Christine Casey on the same phone, and asks, "can you meet me at the airport at seven o'clock, this is very important." He doesn't offer any other information over the telephone. The twins wait anxiously for the time to pick up their mother, when finally their Dad announces, "okay it's time to leave to pick up Mom."

The three of them arrive at the airport, and find a place to park, then go inside the terminal to find Christine. Tom told her to meet him at the baggage claim. They are there only a few minutes when Christine arrives. What's up Tom, your voice had a sound of urgency on the phone." The four of them go to the snack shop, for sodas and coffee. Tom asks Christine, "what do you know about Art Shaw?" She proceeds to say, "he has only been with the bureau for two years, and I don't know his background beyond that." Tom up-dates her about Hud and Rick rescuing Mrs. Winters, and Art's involvement. She asks, "is Lois all right?" Tell me everything. Tom is thinking to himself, we are in real trouble if we can't trust Christine.

Tom relates to Christine, "we don't have any choice, but to trust Hud. There is a leak in the FBI, and I don't know who is involved. Hud has worked for NCIS for years and has a flawless reputation. I feel we have to trust someone, and I think Hud is the right person." Christine agrees with Tom, "I also ran a check on Hud, and his record is without question the best I have ever seen." Tom proceeds to bring Christine up to speed on all of the events that have happened so far. She says, "I now understand why you feel so untrusting of the FBI."

Tom says, "we need to have Art Shaw secretly arrested, and take him off the streets before he attempts to harm someone else. Hud is having a trusted friend drive the two men to Washington that was also involved in Lois's kidnapping. We'll stash the three of them in a secret location, maybe we can get at least one of them to talk." Christine says, "we'll let the word out that I have placed Art on a secret mission, so no one is suspicious of his where-a-bouts. We will stash him somewhere, I was thinking either a FBI safe house or perhaps Hud would know of a NCIS hiding place."

She then asks Tom, for Hud's cell phone number, "I know his cell is not bugged." She finds a pay phone and gets a hold of Hud. When Christine hears Hud's voice her heart skips a beat, and she reminds herself this is not social. She tells him, "I am at the airport with Tom Winters, and he brought me up to date with this case." She asks Hud, "what is your plan for the two thugs you have picked up?" He explains, "I have some NCIS friends that I would trust my life with. My friends have agreed to take them, and hide them in a place that nobody knows about." He repeats the same thing Tom told her, "I don't know who can be trusted at the FBI bureau."

Christine asked, "when are you coming back to Washington?" Hud answers, "I am going to help my friends interrogate the two men that held Lois Winters captive, and then I will take the first available flight back.

What plans do you have for Art Shaw?" She replies, "we need to discuss this when you return to DC." Hud says, "that's fine we'll handle him when I get back. I have one final request before you hang up, get a cell phone, in somebody else's name. Someone who is not involved with the government in any way, then call me immediately with the number." She answers, "consider it done, I'll see you when you get back."

When Rick and his mother arrive at the airport they meet Tom, along with the twins, and Christine as agreed upon at the baggage claim department. The Winters family gathers together as they hug and kiss, and tears of joy are also shed. Christine stood back so they could enjoy this very special re-union. While all of this is going on, she is thinking maybe someday I'll have a family like this. After the hugging and kissing, Tom walks over to Christine, and instructs her, "get some agents, that you know can be trusted, to guard Lois." Christine tells Tom, I'll take care of that right now as she gives Tom a hug and says good bye.

They drive back to the Winters house in Roseville. Mrs. Bellinger and the parrots are at the door waiting for them. The parrots are so excited they have prepared a welcome home song for Mrs. Winters. They sing in perfect harmony, "Everything's Beautiful in its Own Way." The whole family is laughing, and Rick says, "WOW what a day, it seems like old times with mom back home. Lois and Tom look at each other and smile.

When Hud returns to DC, he sets up a lunch meeting with Christine. He tells her, "be very careful you are not followed, I don't want anybody to know I am working on this case."

After lunch Hud and Christine go for a walk and discuss the case. Hud tells her what Rick had said about Robert Stevens, the President's Press Secretary. Christine asks, "how did Rick find out about him? We have been investigating him for a few months, and can't find anything on him." Hud says, "I have to tell you something that you will have trouble believing, but we have to use it to try to get to the bottom of this." Christine looks at Hud curiously, and asks, "what secret would that be?" Hud answers, "I know you have seen Johnny the parrot at the Winters house." "Yes," she says, "he's a chatty little guy, but what would he have to do with the case?" Hud replies, "there's a lot you don't know about Johnny, as he swallows hard, he reads people's minds." Christine asked in a shocked voice, "he does what?" "You heard me right, Johnny reads people's minds." "How is that possible, and how did you find out?" "Johnny was my parrot, I bought him in a pet shop. I went in there to get some food for my fish, and was standing there watching him with amusement. I was thinking about stopping on the way home to get a beer and pizza, when he starts squawking beer and pizza, Johnny wants beer and pizza too. I knew something was different so I bought him. A few weeks after I took him home I had to go to Iraq on an assignment, and left him with my landlady, and they got into a squabble about her last beer. She beat him up and threw him outside, that's when the twins found him and nurtured him back to health." Christine laughs, "wow that's quite a story."

The balance of the summer vacation goes by fast, as Rick is getting ready to return to college. Rick tells his parents, "I need to leave a few days early, to make sure I can make changes in my college courses. I definitely have decided to change my vocation from an attorney, to a private investigator. I also talked to the college student advisor, about making this change, and I was advised that a lot of the courses I have already taken, I will get credit for." Rick is excited to get started with this new career vocation, and leaves for school.

The twins have a few more days before their school opens; Lois takes them to the mall shopping for school clothes. She tells them both; "you have grown like weeds over the summer, so let's get shopping." Jimmy is easy to buy for, he loves pull over shirts and jeans, and Nike tennis shoes. Everything that Jimmy needs in clothes they find at The Old Navy Store. They look for some cute outfits for Amie, but she only finds one outfit she likes. Mrs. Winters tells Amie, "we'll go to a few more stores for the rest of your school clothes, after we go to the shoe store for Jimmy's tennis shoes." Mrs. Winters thinks to herself, that girl sure is into fashion big time. Mrs. Winters says to Amie, "you have to buy everything you need this afternoon, I have pre-service starting tomorrow, and this is the only time we can shop." Jimmy says to his mom, "Amie is going to take forever do you mind if I go to the bookstore and look at some comic books?" "Go ahead Jimmy, we'll meet you in a little while." Amie says to her mom, "I know exactly what I want, and Macy's probably has it." At Macy's the two of them go to the junior department and Amie was right, she ends up with five new outfits she loves. Now all that's left to buy are a few accessories, they meet Jimmy and go onto the next store.

Jimmy runs into Whiz at the mall, and asks his mom; "can I hang out with the Whiz while you and Amie finish shopping?" "Okay, but meet us in front of the arcade in two hours." With that, Amie and her Mom leave to finish shopping.

Whiz and Jimmy head for the snack bar for a coke. With cokes in hand, they find a table with a good view for checking out all of the chicks. Jimmy prepares to sit down and stops abruptly! There sitting directly across from their table is, without a doubt, the most beautiful girl in the world. Jimmy has the urge to walk right up to her, and say something really clever, but noticing the older lady sitting with her, he has second thoughts. Whiz notices Jimmy practically drooling, while looking at the girl. "I can introduce you to her if you want." "You're kidding! You really know her?" "I sure do her name is Sydney Shepard. She's your new neighbor." "How come I haven't seen her before, Jimmy asked?" " I met her when my mom took me to enroll in the after-school karate class. Her mom is the instructor, and Sydney helps with the class." "I have to join that class! I'm in love with her". Whiz laughs. "How about I introduce you to her." "Great", says Jimmy. Whiz waves to Sydney, and the two of them walk over to meet her. Jimmy thinks to himself that she is even more beautiful close up. Whiz makes the introductions and Sydney looks a little embarrassed, and gives Jimmy a shy smile. Mrs. Shepard suggests they share their table. Jimmy trying to act like a macho guy, leans over the table to shake Mrs. Shepard's hand. Unfortunately his coke is in the hand he needs. He becomes flustered, and in the aftermath the coke splashes across the table, causing everyone to jump up. Jimmy rushes to apologize, and grabs his coat sleeve, and attempts to wipe her down. It's okay, she says, "I'm fine, please sit down."

Jimmy unaware that Whiz has moved his chair, starts to sit down, only to end up on the floor, with the remainder of his coke splattered on the floor and himself. Whiz laughing, extends his hand to pull Jimmy back on his feet. In the midst of all the confusion, a cell phone rings. Sydney's mom reaches for her phone, her elbow brushes the glass of iced tea in front of her, and once again the table is flooded. Now this awkward situation has the whole group roaring with laughter. Jimmy and Mrs. Shepard look at each other, and Mrs. Shepard says, "Jimmy I think we are two of a kind" and they all start laughing again.

Whiz and Sydney begin talking about their up-coming karate lesson on Monday after school. Mrs.

Shepard asks Jimmy, "have you thought about enrolling in the karate class with Whiz?" "My dad suggested awhile ago that my twin sister Amie, and I should join a self-defense class. When I get home I will ask him to sign the enrollment form that was provided by the school." Mrs. Shepard says, "great, get to school early on Monday to drop off the form. Well young lady Mrs. Shepard says, we had better finish our shopping so you will be ready for classes on Monday." Whiz and Jimmy say their good-byes. Sydney smiles sweetly, "I'll see you two on Monday."

Whiz and Jimmy rush back to the arcade, they are a little late to meet Jimmy's mom. When Jimmy sees his mom, he runs up to her to tell her about meeting the new neighbor girl. Mrs. Winters remarks, "Jimmy, I have never seen you so excited about a girl before." "I know mom, but this girl is special."

When they get home Jimmy immediately finds the karate class enrollment form, and asks his dad, if he and Amie can enroll for this class. Mr. Winter replies, "son I think that would be a fine idea."

The first day of school is exciting, as the twins meet up with all of their school chums, and everyone is talking about their summer vacations. They also meet a couple new teachers that weren't there last year, and see several new students.

They are both excited about their first karate class lesson after school in the gymnasium. As Jimmy's good luck continues, he gets to pair up with Sydney their very first lesson. He knows she is going to kick his butt, because Whiz mentioned she has been taking lessons for two years, but he doesn't care, being close to her is exciting enough. And his thinking was right, the first move BAM on his back he went, looking up at her he asks, "how long will it take for me to be that good?" Sydney says, "I think I can whip you into shape in one semester." Jimmy looks up smiling, "I was hoping it would take longer then that," as Sydney smiles back sensing excitement in Jimmy's voice.

Jimmy looks around the gym to see how the Whiz is doing, and sees his partner is throwing him around like a piece of meat. Whiz starts screaming like a girl, and the whole class bursts out laughing. Mrs. Shepard claps her hands to get the class attention and points to Sierra, who is Whiz's partner and tells her, "go easy on Whiz." This starts the whole class laughing again. Mrs. Shepard claps her hands; "okay class get serious, and practice the karate moves that I have shown you."

Amie's partner is Kevin Hunt. Amie and Kevin had talked before the class began and she is thinking this guy is a real hunk. Amie says to Kevin, "you look familiar to me." Kevin asks, "don't you remember me? I used to play with you and Jimmy when we were younger." "Oh, yeah your Mrs. Hunt's nephew, I didn't recognize you at first."

Jimmy sees Amie and smiles; and she gives him the thumbs up. Jimmy can see that Amie's partner is happy to be paired up with her.

After class, the six kids decide to walk home together, and they are all discussing the fun of the karate class. They start walking as couples, and this is when Sydney decides to ask Jimmy to the up and coming Sadie Hawkins dance. She takes a deep breath, and thinks here I go. "Jimmy would you like to go to the dance with me?" Jimmy answers quickly, "YES would I ever!" Sydney breathes a sigh of relief, and gives Jimmy a big smile, "great, I was afraid some one else had already asked you." Whiz overhears their conversation. "I have a great idea, why don't we all go to the Sadie Hawkins dance together?" Amie asks Kevin, "would you like to go with me, Kevin says, "sounds like a winner to me." Whiz interrupts "by the way, what is a Sadie Hawkins dance?" Jimmy says, "for being such a smart guy, there is a lot you don't know. Amie would you explain to our genius friend, what a Sadie Hawkins dance is?" Amie tells Whiz, "the girls are supposed to invite the boys to the dance." Whiz interrupts again, and asks Sierra, "are you going to ask me." Sierra laughs and answers, "of course, I'm going to invite you." Whiz says, "whew, I'm glad that's settled." Amie continues explaining to the group, "we all dress up in old fashion square dancing clothes, and there is going to be a square dance caller on hand, with a local band providing the music." "My mom is going to be the dance instructor, and this is going to be a real blast, Sydney says." The girls start talking about the cute outfits they are going to put together. The boys all agree to dress in jeans and cowboy shirts, and look for straw hats to wear. Too soon they are at the Winters house, Amie says "we are not going to have dinner for awhile, come on in and have a coke."

When they enter the Winters household Mr. Winters greets the crowd of eighth graders. Tom tells the group, "I received a phone call from the school requesting for Johnny and Barbie to perform a couple of songs, at the Sadie Hawkins dance." Sydney looks at Jimmy and asks, "who are Johnny and Barbie?" Jimmy answers, "oh that's right, you don't know about our talented parrots. They are practically worldwide entertainers, maybe I'm exaggerating, but they are very good. Come on upstairs and meet the crazy birds." The group runs upstairs, and you can hear the parrots singing. They sound like Kenny Rogers and Dolly Parton singing Islands in the Sky. When they walk into the computer room, the two birds quit singing, and stare at Sydney. Johnny who is always being a smartie, "whistles at Sydney, and then asks Jimmy, "where did you find this beautiful babe?" Jimmy says to Sydney, "this is Johnny and Barbie." They both bow and Johnny asks, "do you want to hear some Elvis?" Sydney says, "sure would, he is my all time favorite." They both sing Don't Be Cruel, and Teddy Bear. Sydney claps when they are done, "Wow you two are--really good."

Mrs. Bellinger calls from downstairs; "I have some cokes and chips down here for you kids." They run downstairs where they meet Mrs. Winters, who has just arrived home from teaching school, and Jimmy introduces her to Sydney. Mrs. Winters asks, "what brings you to Roseville?" "My mother is a karate teacher, and we are from Holt Michigan. My mother worked for the Holt School District, as an instructor, and my dad works for General Motors. He is the one that got transferred. Dad has a sister that lives in Roseville, and she found the house down the street for us. My dad has quite a commute to DC every day to his job." Mrs. Winters says, "I'm also driving back and forth too." Mr. Winters adds, "I did it for a long time before I got hurt."

Sydney notices that Mr. Winters is on crutches, and asks what happened? He says to make a long story short, "I was run over by a hit and run driver. I'm on the mend now; I just need some more therapy." Amie says, "pretty soon dad will be good as new."

The kids finish their refreshments, and Jimmy and Amie walk their friends to the door. Sydney asks Jimmy, "I hate to seem nosy, but I can't help but wonder who the big burly men are in your house?" Jimmy tells her, "that's another long story," he quickly makes up a story telling her all FBI agents have bodyguards. He didn't want to tell her about his mom's kidnapping, as he is afraid of scaring her away. Sydney looks a little shocked after finding out that Mr. Winters works for the FBI. "Are you guys in danger or any thing like that?" Don't worry Jimmy says, "the FBI is being cautious, we are not in any danger." Whiz says to Sydney, "just don't spend the night here," and both Jimmy and Amie give him the look. Sydney asks, "what do you mean don't spend the night here?" Whiz, after getting the evil eye from the twins, says, "I'm just kidding.

The school week went by fast for the twins, but they have a lot of homework, more now that they are in the eighth grade. Homework is a big priority in the Winters household, so they have not had much time to socialize. Although they both have been on the phone a lot, and the six of them meet everyday at the school cafeteria for lunch, to talk over their plans for the dance. At last Friday is here, and the twins rush home from school, to get ready for the big dance.

The Winters household is full of hustle and bustle as the twins quickly eat their dinner. You can hear Johnny and Barbie singing in the background. They too, are excited about the dance. Mrs. Winters earlier in the week, went to the local costume shop, and found straw hats and cowboy shirts, for all of the boys and a straw hat for Johnny from the toy store.

Mrs. Bellinger found some material to make Amie's skirt. "Oh Mrs. Bellinger thank you, this is so beautiful." The skirt was gathered at the waist, showing off Amie's small waistline, and full at the bottom, and the length is just below her knees. As she spins around the room, the skirt gently flows with her. Amie exclaims, "you remembered my favorite color is pink." The color of the skirt is shades of pinks, running from a light pink, to a bright bold rose with a matching top. Mrs. Winters walks in the room and says to Amie, "you look absolutely beautiful." Amie blushes, and gives Mrs. Bellinger a kiss on the cheek, and thanks her again.

Tom and Lois are downstairs, as the other children arrive. Lois has her camera out snapping pictures of them. Everyone is talking at once and the boys are showing off, acting like they are old time cowboys. It had earlier been decided that Mrs. Winters would drive them to the school, and Sydney's mom will drop everyone off after the dance.

Johnny and Barbie are riding in the band's limousine. A few of the band members are also in the limo, the lead singer asks Johnny to do his famous Elvis impression. Johnny is happy to show off, and sings his favorite; You Ain't Nothing But A Hound Dog. "Dang, the lead singer says to Johnny, you sing better than I do."

When they step out of the car, they can hear the music playing loudly. As they are walking in Amie remarks, "it looks like our whole class is here." Sydney exclaims, "look how cute all the girls look." Whiz whistles, "wow their cute all right, but not as cute as our dates." Jimmy says, "let's get in there, and show them our stuff."

The parrots are sitting at the front of the stage. The band is playing a fast country song originally sang by Brooks and Dunn named "Boot Scootin' Boogie." The girls in their full skirts are twirling and laughing. This is something new for the school, usually the music provided to the school dances are the current songs that are played on the radio. Everyone is enjoying themselves and doing their best to do the country-dances.

Mrs. Shepard talks into the mike and announces, "it is time to do a few square dances." She asks her daughter, "come on the stage, and bring your friends with you." Mrs. Shepard invites one other couple to join them on stage, so they have a group of four couples dancing. The four couples reluctantly walk on stage ready for their lesson. The other kids are told by Mrs. Shepard to get into groups of four couples, with the girls standing to the left of the boys, now they are ready to begin. She begins by explaining to them, the promenade, dosey doe, allemande left, allemande right. Most of the kids have never squared danced before, and Mrs. Shepard thinks to herself, this is going to be a long night. Finally the kids have mastered some of the steps, and the music begins with the dancers whirling around the gym, giggling as they dance. Whiz and Sierra are dancing, and the Whiz is yelling "Hee Haw." Mrs. Shepard looks at them and thinks to herself, something looks wrong with the way they are dancing, and she realizes that Whiz in on the wrong side of Sierra.

Now it's time for the parrots to sing their duet, as the kids are cheering and clapping when the parrots are introduced. Johnny is wearing a straw hat, and Barbie has on an old fashion bonnet with a skirt that Mrs. Bellinger made for her. They start singing a Kenny Rogers and Dolly Parton song, "Islands In The Sky." The two of them have rehearsed this song all week, and they perform it flawlessly. The kids show their appreciation by yelling, "encore, encore." The bandleader asks the parrots if they are prepared to do another song? Johnny replies, "are we ever" as they start singing a Faith Hill and Tim McGraw ballad, "I'm In Love with you." Johnny and Barbie look so cute singing this love song; as they gaze into each other eyes, just like Faith and Tim do, when they sing this song together. At the end of the song they take their bows and Johnny says, as he usually does when his performance is over, his Elvis impression of "thank you very much ladies and gentlemen." Barbie pipes in and tells the laughing crowd, "Elvis has left the building."

The dance is over too soon, and the kids file out of the gym. The six kids and Mrs. Shepard, along with the parrots go to her car for the drive home. They stop at the Stone Cold Ice Creamery, and Johnny tells them," Barbie and I want a cup of ice cream too." Jimmy says, "okay," and puts Johnny on his shoulder. Amie grabs Barbie and puts her onto her shoulder. What a sight Mrs. Shepard thinks, as she shakes her head, the kids and the parrots dressed in square dance clothes. She chuckles to herself, as this peculiar looking entourage walk into the ice cream store. The clerk looks twice at them, and Johnny asks her, "what are you staring at, haven't you ever waited on a parrot before?" The attendant repeats back, "not one with a straw hat on." Everybody laughs. It was a wonderful night to be remembered by all.

Time has gone by fast, and it is election time in three weeks. The President has a huge lead in the polls over

David Ferris. Robert Stevens, the Press secretary tells his associates, "something needs to be done, and done now." His right-hand man tells him, "don't worry my men and I will take care of the situation," Robert Stevens says, "it had better happen or else."

Two days later the Winters family is having supper, when the evening news comes on television. They hear the terrible news that the President's helicopter is missing, with the President on board. The White House Press secretary says, "the satellite navigation system on board the plane, doesn't seem to be working. The plane went off radar somewhere in West Virginia, and all available planes, and helicopters are searching the mountains in the area." Tom Winters clearly upset, tells his family, "what a terrible tragedy to happen." The twins are crying, and Tom tells them, "we can't give up hope, maybe the President will be found alive. He adds, I bet this has something to do with all of the other things that have been happening."

After two days of searching, the White House announces the President's helicopter has been located, and the plane has been severely burnt and no survivors have been found. The newscaster is saying over and over, "the fear is the President is dead." Just as everyone feared Robert Stevens the Presidents Press Secretary confirms the sad news the President is now declared dead.

Tom Winters after calming his family down, excuses himself, and tells his family, he is going to his office to catch up on some paper work. When he reaches his office, he closes the door, and immediately calls Hud and Christine, to set up an emergency meeting with them.

Mr. Winters invites Hud and Christine over for some chocolate cake, and coffee. That was the agreed upon code, when Tom needed to meet with them, about this high profile case. He is using a cell phone that no one knows he has; as he feels the need to be very careful, especially now that the President has been declared dead. Hud responds to Tom saying, "I would love to have something sweet to eat, chocolate is my favorite. I don't have a great cook like Mrs. Bellinger, beside I haven't seen Johnny in awhile, and I miss him. I'll have Christine pick me up, and we'll see you shortly." Christine arrives, and the two of them drive the short distance to the Winters house

The kids are surprised to see Hud, and Christine, but they welcome the unexpected company, to take their minds off the fact, the President is dead. When Johnny hears Hud's voice, both he and Barbie fly down the stairs. Johnny is squawking, "Hud, Hud where have you been?" Hud tells him, "calm down, I just live down the street if you need to talk to me." Johnny by now is perched on Hud's shoulder, and Barbie is looking adoringly at the two of them, and the whole tribe goes into the living room.

Since the President's plane has gone down, the television news has been on non-stop. A news reporter interrupts the program in session; the President's Press Secretary is about to give a speech. There is complete silence in the Winters household, as Robert Steven's appears on TV. He begins by reassuring all Americans; the country is in good hands, with Vice President Truman Bridges.

Robert Stevens introduces the Vice President, who has been sworn in as the President of the United States.

After the long speech by Truman Bridges, Robert Stevens appears back on the television. He introduces a man named David Ferris, who will be running for President. Christine, Tom, and Hud look at each other, and Hud says, "this is very strange," he would put that man on television, this early after the President has died."

David Ferris starts by saying how sorry he is about the President, but the country must move on, and he is the man for the job. The whole family is shocked by this intrusion, so early after the President's death.

Johnny starts yelling, "bad man- bad man," everybody looks at Johnny and Hud asks, "what's up boy?" Johnny replies, "you are not going to believe this!" Johnny is staring intently at the Press Secretary, again he says. "You are not going to believe this." "Johnny will you please, tell us what is going on?" "Whoopee, Johnny squawks, the President is still alive!" Mr. Winters asks "are you sure?" "Yes, yes the whole plane crash was staged by Robert Stevens, and David Ferris and his colleagues."

Hud says, "thinking back when I was at the scene of the crash to investigate, it was suspicious to me about the lack of body parts, I put that down in my notes. However, it is feasible that wild animals carried the bones away, but I remember thinking at the time, it was very strange." Christine asked, "are you kidding? Are you going to take the word of a bird?" Hud says, "I know it's hard to believe that Johnny reads minds, but in the past he has stopped a lot of crimes with his gift." Mr. Winters says," in the short time Johnny has been with us, he has helped to prevent several crimes, if it wasn't for him, we probably would not have gotten the kids mother back. He also helped to get the Whiz kid back. Believe me, we have to take Johnny very seriously,"

After all the cheering, laughing and hugging, Christine looks at Johnny, "wow what a way to solve the world's problems. Would you like to ride around with me every day, we could catch all the bad guys?" she asked. Johnny replies." I have to stay and protect Barbie." Hud speaks in a stern voice, and says "we cannot tell anybody about what we just heard or we would all be in real danger."

Barbie looks at Johnny, "you are my hero" as they dance around singing, "God Bless America" in perfect harmony. Johnny struts around, trying to impress Barbie even more, as she is cooing like a school girl in love. Christine is thinking how nice it is for them to be in love. Hud reminds him, "we still have a lot of work to do and I am going to need a lot more help from you, are you with me?" Johnny replies, "I'll do anything you ask boss."

Johnny flies over to Hud, and asks, "what's our next move?" Hud is thinking aloud, "obviously he says, they had an opportunity to kill the President, and they didn't. So that tells me they don't want him dead. But what is it they are trying to accomplish?" Tom says, "it must have something to do with the up-and coming elections in November." Christine speaks with excitement, "that's it! I have noticed Stevens and Ferris have been real tight lately. One of my top agents reported to me, they thought the two of them have been acting very secretively." Hud says,"good, now were getting somewhere." He also goes on to say, "so if they stashed the President somewhere, and everybody thinks he is dead, that gives them a chance to put David Ferris in office." The three of them agree this is the reason they staged the accident. "We must find a way to stop them," Hud states firmly.

"The first thing we have to do is find out where the President is being held, and get him back to the White House before the elections," Hud says. Christine adds, "we need to put a tail on Ferris and Stevens, but I don't want to use any of our FBI agents, because I'm sure there are more rotten agents involved. This whole caper would take a lot of agents to pull off." She then asks Hud, "do you have any available N.C.I.S men that you can trust with your life?" "My men are untouchable when it comes to being involved in corruption." Hud asks Tom, "how many men do you think I should put on?" Tom answers,

"I think if we had ten good men, we could outsmart these scoundrels." Hud says, "I will round up my crew in the morning. When we get our men together, then we'll decide who else may be involved with this scheme, and have them followed. Our ace in the hole is, we have Johnny. We can take him into the White House with us, and try to meet with Ferris and Stevens. We can explain that Johnny is with us because he is an expert at finding human remains. We'll ask them if they would like to use Johnny's services? Of course they'll say no, meanwhile Johnny can try to read their minds for clues to where the President is." "Hud you are a genius, they'll have to meet with you, to give the appearance they really want the President's body found, otherwise people might get suspicious," Christine said.

Christine is yawning as Hud looks at his watch, and says, "it's really getting late. Christine we should get going, so we can get an early start in the morning." "I had no idea it was so late, Tom agreed. Johnny, you and Barbie better get to bed, and get a good night's sleep. We will be using your help to find the President." Johnny squawks," I'll do anything you ask to save our President." Hud smiles, "Johnny you are a real trouper."

The next morning Hud is up early, and already he and Christine have talked, on the phone. Hud is working on rounding up his crew of NCIS men to help find the President. Christine has called the White House trying to arrange a meeting with Robert Stevens, but because it is Saturday, Stevens is not at the White House. His secretary doesn't work on the weekend, and she has the telephone recorder on. Christine leaves a message, but it is doubtful that her call will be returned soon. Hud calls Tom Winters and reports that he is getting his men set up, but they are having a problem getting a hold of Stevens to set up a meeting.

Over breakfast, Tom, and the children are talking about taking Johnny with them to meet with Stevens, but at the time they are having a hard time contacting him to arrange a meeting. The twins look at each other, and quickly finish their breakfast, and ask their dad if they can be excused. Tom says to them, "you two need to eat more slowly, but yes, you are excused."

They run up the stairs to the computer room, and Amie calls the Whiz to tell him to get over here right away. The Whiz answers, "I'm still in bed, Sierra and I practiced our karate last night, and that girl is wicked, she is scaring me with all of her karate moves." Jimmy grabs the phone and tells him, "I don't care if you were up all night, and Sierra broke all of your bones, get over here pronto." "Okay you don't have to get an attitude, I'll be right there, have the coffee ready for me." Jimmy says, "Whiz you don't drink coffee," and he laughs, "that's right I don't, but how about a cup of hot chocolate." "You got it, just hurry up"

Whiz, for being so tired gets to the Winters home in a short time. Mr. Winters answers the door, and remarks to the Whiz, "you certainly are up early for a Saturday morning," and the Whiz says, "mornings are my best time." Mr. Winters looks at him, and thinks to himself, that boy sure is an odd one, he chuckles as he watches the Whiz run upstairs.

Whiz enters the room and tells the twins, "this had better be good." Amie says, "it is, but you have to swear not to tell anyone." Whiz crosses his heart, "I swear, even if Sierra threatens me I won't tell." "Well you better sit down, and when I tell you, don't make a sound, we don't want dad to know that we told you." "Come on spit it out, it's not like you are going to tell me the President is alive or something like that." Amie and Jimmy look at each other, and Whiz says, "that's it, isn't it? The President really is alive." Jimmy puts his hand over Whiz's mouth so no one can hear, and he shakes his head yes. Whiz and the twins Hi-Five, and the Whiz says, "that's so cooolll dude. How did you discover this miracle? Oh I know, Johnny discovered it right." "That's right," Jimmy says, "the Press Secretary, Robert Stevens is behind all of this, and we are going to need your help." Whiz gets a scared look on his face and says "not me man I've already been kidnapped, crammed in a trunk, and then stuffed into a closet with two big scary dudes guarding me, and I thought they were going to kill me." Jimmy says, "calm down, we didn't know those thugs were so dangerous. Now we know, and we'll be more careful. Besides we'll be with you, trust me nothing is going to happen to you." "I sure would feel better if Sierra was with me, her karate moves could get me out of any life threatening situation." "Well, you can't tell Sierra. Don't worry Rick is on his way home from college for the weekend and he is going to help us." Whiz asks, "why doesn't that make me feel safer?" Amie gets into the discussion, and tells the Whiz, "quit your whining your gonna be fine. Jimmy, tell Whiz our plan, while he is still breathing," and the three of them laugh. Whiz says, "okay but, if I get kidnapped again, my parents will ground me for life." "Jimmy tells him, "this plan is so smooth your parents will not know a thing about it." Amie goes over and hugs Whiz, "thank you, you are our best friend we are not going to let anything happen to you."

Whiz says, "okay shoot what's the plan?" "First you need to find the address of Robert Stevens," Amie explains, "Jimmy and I tried to find it on the computer but it comes up classified." Hmm, Whiz mumbles, "that's not a problem I can get that in no time." Amie says, "well there's the computer get busy." The Whiz almost immediately has the address. He prints it out and tells Amie in a cocky voice, "the back door way into their computer is tricky, but not for this kid, what's next?" Amie says to Whiz, "that's great, we tried over an hour to find it, and still didn't have any luck."

Amie tells Jimmy, "go ahead and explain our plan further." "We are going to put Satellite Chips in our shoes so our dad can find us if something goes wrong. Whiz if you get kidnapped dad will find you in a hurry." Whiz replies, "why do I feel like something is going to go wrong." Amie says to him, "you are gun shy after your last experience, believe us, everything is going to go like clock work."

Jimmy goes on to explain, "the next thing is to have Rick take Johnny with us, to the Stevens house after dark." Whoa Whiz says, "I have a question, why isn't Hud or the FBI taking care of this?" Jimmy answers, "they tried but they have to follow proper procedure, and for us that's not fast enough. They are having a problem setting up a meeting with Stevens." Amie says, "we feel that we need to do something right away, before something else happens to the President."

As soon as Rick arrives home, the twins go running down the stairs to greet him. "Come on up to the computer room Rick," Amie says, "we want to show you what we are working on." "Give me a minute, I want to talk to Mom and Dad." "Okay but hurry up." Rick hurriedly gives his mom and dad a hug, and they talk for a few minutes. He tells his parents "I need to go see what the twins are up to."

When Rick gets upstairs the three of them are talking all at once, and Rick says, "please one at a time, I can't make out a word you are saying." Jimmy starts talking, "okay you two, let me talk," as he goes on to bring Rick up to speed about the President, and what their plan is. "Just a minute," Rick said, "before you guys go any further with your plan to visit the Stevens house, don't you think we should clear this with dad? I think we would all be in danger no matter what precautions we take." Whiz jumps in, "see I told you guys we could get killed." Jimmy says,

"Rick we have Johnny to rely on." Rick shakes his head, and tells the anxious group, "remember Johnny has been seen on television, they might recognize him." "Really Rick," Amie says, "all parrots look alike. We can do this, and be back home in a couple of hours, and no one will be the wiser." "Okay, you guys, you have convinced me, besides I have a few tricks up my sleeve."

They all go traipsing downstairs, and Amie says to her folks, "we are going out for ice cream if it's okay." Lois Winters looks at Tom and says, "I think that's innocent enough, what do you think? Besides the FBI will be behind them." Tom gives them permission, "okay go have a good time, but be back in a couple of hours."

On the way out, Whiz picks up a satchel he left in the bushes in front of the Winters house, he doesn't want the kids parents to see all the stuff he has. Amie asks the Whiz, "what do you have in the old satchel?" "I'll tell you all about it later."

They jump in Rick's Mustang with Johnny on Rick's shoulder, squawking, "I love ice cream. Rick can we bring Barbie back some ice cream too?" "Sure we'll get her anything you want," and Johnny says, "good, I gotta take care of my girl." Rick says, "I never get used to you talking like a human." "I know I surprise myself."

Amie again, asks the Whiz, "just what stuff do you have in that bag?" "Okay I'll show you he says." Whiz unzips the bag, and dumps everything on the seat. He takes the huge flashlight that was included in the bag, "let me explain what all this apparatus is." The flashlight is the brightest flashlight the twins have ever seen. It lights up the entire interior of the car. Rick yells, "hold that light down it is blurring my vision." Whiz says, "sorry Rick," and continues on talking about the different devices that is built into the flashlight. "Look he says, it has a special cell phone on the side of it, that is to be used after we stick the GPS onto the Press Secretary's car, it will also tap into his car phone." "Neat", Amie says, "but where did you get all of this stuff?" Whiz replies, "after my kidnapping, and my near death, I started reading spy magazines, and discovered that you can order all kinds of spy equipment from them. But let me finish explaining what else this flashlight is. At the end of it is a camera, and you don't have to have the light on for it to work. On the other end is a lock picker that is guaranteed to pick any lock. The radio is also a recording device. I felt like I had to get something to protect myself if I was going to hang out with you guys." Jimmy laughs and asks the Whiz, "are you getting a little paranoid?" Whiz says, "let me explain what the rest of the flashlight does." Rick yells back, "it even does more! How much did you pay for all of that?" "I have been saving my allowance for years and my grandparents for every birthday, gave me a thousand dollars so I used a big chunk of that." Whiz goes on to say, "the flashlight even has a mini computer when you flip the flashlight over, and slide out the drawer, just like magic a keyboard appears. It's also equipped with a siren too if we need to make a lot of noise." Jimmy says, "I guess you are ready for our next caper."

Whiz tells Rick, "head for the gated community of Monterey." Rick says, "that's all I need to know for now, when we get in the area I'll park the car to go over our plans. Is everyone buckled up, because now is the time to lose our FBI friends." Johnny yells, "hang onto your butt here we go," as Rick squeals the Mustang's tires making an unexpected sharp turn off the freeway. Jimmy looks behind, "good move, the agents kept on going." Rick says, "great now we are going to get back on the freeway, and they won't know what direction we are going." Rick slowly turns the car around, and enters the freeway, and follows it to exit ninety-six. "This strip mall looks like a good place to map out our scheme." He parks the car, and turns the engine off with Johnny squawking, telling Rick, "squeal the tires some more, that was fun". Rick laughs, "Johnny are you trying to get me a ticket?" Whiz tells Johnny, "we don't need to cause attention, especially with all of my spy equipment in the car, the cops will think we are robbers."

Rick parks the car, and tells Whiz, "turn on your James Bond flashlight, and give me the exact address of the Press Secretary." Whiz hands him the address, and at the same time Rick pulls out his laptop, to find the location of his house.

Rick also grabs his notebook, Amie asks, "wow Rick what is all of this stuff?" Rick answers, "well sweetie, the Whiz isn't the only one that has come prepared, I have a lot of other stuff in the trunk, but I'll get to that after I go over everyone's assignment." Jimmy says, "good Amie and I have been practicing our karate, so we are prepared to do anything you ask."

Rick points to the map on the computer and tells the kids, "this is where we are at, and this is the Press Secretary's house. I'm going to send Johnny to scope out the Stevens house. He is going to be our look out." Johnny replies, "look out bad guys here I come." Jimmy says, "that's right Johnny, that's the idea." Rick continues, "Johnny you are going to fly to the Stevens house and see who is there. I will also need to know what part of the house the occupants are in. If possible let me know how many people are in the house." Johnny flies out of the car singing, "look out you bad guys here I come," to the tune of The Lonesome Road. Jimmy says, "shh Johnny be quiet we don't want anyone to hear you." "Okay, boss I'll shut up." Rick tells Johnny, "we'll be waiting right here for you."

While Johnny is scouting the Stevens house, Rick and the twins, and Whiz go over the directions on how to get to the house and return to the car. Jimmy who is usually on the quiet side tells Rick, "Amie and I have the directions all figured out." Whiz jokes, that part is pretty easy, I think we are ready to hear our real jobs." Okay Rick tells them, "I just don't want anything to happen to any of you. We are going to separate and everyone is going to have to know how to get back to the car. Jimmy and Amie, I want you to go up to the guard shack and tell him you are looking for your dog." Whiz butts in, "what is the dog's name?" Rick said, "call him anything you want, but let me go on with our plan. While you two are distracting the guard, Whiz and I will climb the wall to get into the sub-division. Amie we all know how dramatic you can be so this is the time to use it." Amie says, "I don't know what you mean about being dramatic." Jimmy pipes up, "sure you do, you act that way all the time."

Rick interrupts them, and tells the twins, "you can continue the sibling rivaling later, right now pay attention to business. After you two get to the guard shack, I want you to pretend you are calling your dog, and ask the guard if you can go inside the gate to look for your dog. The Stevens house is the first house to the right of the guard shack, so when you get into the gate, walk to the left of the guard shack, that will get his attention looking toward you and away from the Stevens house." Amie says to Jimmy, "let's call our imaginary dog Chancy." He says, "I like that name, we will tell the guard he is a black and white English Cocker Spaniel, like our grandma Nan had." "Good idea," Amie says. Rick tells them, "now you're cooking, who could turn you two down, the guard will have to let you in."

While Rick is talking the Whiz puts on his spy hat. It looks like a motorcycle helmet with a flashlight attached to it. Inside the hat it has a compartment with a rope in it. The Winters kids look at Whiz, and Rick says to him, "what the heck is the helmet for?" Whiz replies, "that's the beauty of it, look at the inside of my helmet," as he removes it from his head. Whiz shows Rick, "all I have to do is push this button and a rope will shoot out of this compartment, we will need the rope to scale the wall to the gated community." Rick agrees, "it will make our job easier getting up the wall, good planning Whiz. We can't have the light on when we go up the wall, the guard will surely see us." Whiz replies, "oh yeah I didn't think of that."

Johnny comes flying back to the car, just as Rick is explaining to the Whiz what the two of them are going to do after climbing the wall. Johnny is out of breath, "boss no one is home at the Stevens house. I flew around the house twice, and I looked in all of the windows and I didn't see a soul inside or outside."

Rick says, "that's great; our job will be much easier. Lets get going; this little job shouldn't take long," while the anxiety in his stomach is telling him different.

The twins walk up to the guard shack, and Amie has big crocodile tears in her eyes. Jimmy explains to the guard, "we are looking for our little dog named Chancy." Amie tells the man in between sobs, "he is a black and white English Cocker." She asks, "have you seen him?" The guard looks at her and says, "I sure haven't but I'll keep my eyes open for him." Jimmy asks, "can my sister and I have permission to enter through the gate to look for Chancy." "Okay, I'll give you fifteen minutes to look, and if you're not back I will send the security car to look for you." Amie still with big tears in her eyes says to the guard, "thank you so much, we promise we'll be back on time." They enter through the gate calling Chancy as the guard looks on.

All the while the twins are distracting the guard Rick and Whiz are scaling the wall, they are barely breathing as they quietly climb over the wall. Whiz whispers, "that part was easy, now lets stay in the shadows until we get to the garage." They head in the opposite direction of the twins to the Stevens house. Once there, Whiz takes his flashlight, and the lock pick set out, and quickly picks the lock on the garage door, of the four-car garage. As they go into the garage, Rick pats him on the shoulder. Whiz mumbles, "that went great, for the first time I've ever broken into anything," and now his heart is slowing down a bit. They plant the GPS devices under the fender well of both cars that are in the garage. Rick says in a low tone, "I wish all of their cars were here." Whiz says, "I have a good feeling these cars will gives us some good leads."

As they go back to the large fence and climb over, the security guard is back in his office, and he sees two guys running away from the fence on his television monitor, He runs outside and orders them to stop, just as Amie and Jimmy are walking back to the car. The man approaches Whiz and Rick, "halt, and wait right there for the police." He grabs at them, and the Whiz screams, Rick, do something quick." At the same time the twins come running back to see what they can do to help. Now all four kids are there and the twins start using karate on the man, as Rick and Whiz get the rope. Jimmy surprises the guard and throws him over his shoulder onto the ground. The guard gets back on his feet, and Amie jumps on his back yelling Kung Foo stuff. The guard is trying to get her off of him. Jimmy sees his chance and gives the unsuspecting guard a karate chop that knocks his breath away, and he immediately goes down on the ground, giving Rick enough time to tie him up with their rope. Rick says to his crew, "run you guys hurry while the guard is down, and get to the car before the cops come." They all run like they never have before. Amie looks back, "sorry mister I hope we didn't hurt you, someday we'll explain everything." Rick tells her, "quit apologizing to the guard, and get to the car so we can get out here pronto." His adrenaline is running full force, as he turns the corner on two wheels. Once they get back on the freeway, they all let out a gasp at the same time. Jimmy sighs, "that was a close call." Amie still out of breath says, "that was not only a close call, but it was terrifying, I never want to do that again." Whiz and Jimmy are both trying to act cool in front of Amie, and Jimmy tells her, "that job was like a duck swimming in water." Whiz joins in, talking in a high-pitched voice saying, "yeah I wasn't worried for a second."

Amie, asks Whiz, "if you weren't worried why does your voice sound like a girl?" Whiz replies, "I just have a frog in it," Amie giggles, " SURE Whiz. I really hope we didn't hurt the guard." Rick tells her, "don't worry about him, we just got lucky. As big as he is, it would take a freight train to injure him."

Johnny had stayed in the car, and asks the trio about their conversation. He remarks, "that's all it takes for you guys to start shaking and sweating." Rick says, "you would be sweating too if you pulled off a caper like the one we just did." Johnny says, "what's a caper I have not heard that word before." Amie says in a loud voice, "that's when you almost get into a lot of trouble and get thrown in jail." With that the tension is leaving them, and they all start laughing, mostly with relief that everything went okay.

Jimmy asks Rick, "when we get close to home can we stop and get some ice cream?" Johnny reminds them, "I promised my girl Barbie I would bring her back some too." Rick answers, "we'll stop at our favorite ice cream joint, and the ice cream is on me. I think we have all earned it." Whiz says, "I think that's the least you can do for risking our lives." Amie looks at him, "you were fine, we didn't get you kidnapped or anything." He replies, "you're right, I should thank my lucky stars for that."

Rick pulls into the Baskins Robbins and he can see the FBI is following them again. When they park, Rick walks over to apologize to them, "I promise, I will not try to lose you guys again." The FBI agent sternly warns him, "you better not, or you will be grounded at home." Rick tells the kids, "hurry and order your ice cream, I think we should get home fast, as the FBI agents aren't very happy with us."

The next day the kids leave the house to pick up Whiz, then Rick heads for DC. When they get close, the GPS device they planted in one of Stevens cars, shows the car is moving in the direction of the marina. They follow the signal to the marina, and the nearer they get the louder the beep. Whiz says, "you would think they would get more original, and stay away from the marina where they hid me when I was kidnapped." Rick comments, "there is a whole ocean out there, it is a perfect place to get someone out of the country, or hide someone without being noticed." When they arrive at the marina, Rick says, "duck down so you aren't noticed," and Rick puts on his hat and sunglasses for a disguise. He needn't worry about being seen by them, as they are very deep in a conversation, and they are not paying attention to anything going on around them. Rick tells the kids, "you can sit up now, the coast is clear." Rick sees Robert Stevens get into a speedboat with another man, and the two men head out into the large bay. Whiz quickly gets out his binoculars and watches as the craft reaches a large yacht. Rick says, "That could be where they are keeping the President, and I need to call Hud right away." He dials Hud on his cell phone, and luckily he answers immediately. Rick tells him what they have just observed. Hud is overjoyed these kids are smart enough to discover where the President might be, and his gut tells him he had better pay attention to them. Hud asks, "how did you find out where he is being held?" Rick replies, "we planted GPS devices in their cars." "Good job you guys, you should all be detectives."

Hud tells Rick, "we can't do anything till it is dark. I will get my men together and meet you back at the marina at Seven p.m., and you guys go hang out somewhere and have lunch, and I will see you at the entrance to the marina."

The four kids and Johnny drive away from the marina, as Rick looks at his watch, "we have three hours to kill, what would you guys like to do?" Amie replies, " I have an idea, let's call Kevin, Sydney and Sierra to see if we can meet at the mall." "Great idea" Whiz says, "we all need halloween costumes for the dance coming up at the school." Rick cuts in, "good idea we can have lunch at the food court in the mall." The kids immediately get on their cell phone to call their friends to meet at the south DC mall.

They wolf down their lunch and Rick says, "I'm going down to Radio Shack to see what interesting new gadgets they have, and you guys meet me at McDonald's no later than Six o'clock." When the other three kids arrive, all six kids trot down to the Costume Shop. Amie suggests to Kevin, "wouldn't it be cute if we dressed up like couples?" Kevin replies, "what do you mean like couples?" Amie says, "don't you guys get it? "For instance Kevin," as Amie continues talking "we could dress like Herman and Lillie Munster." Sierra yells to Whiz, "yeah you could dress up like Superman, and I could be your girlfriend Lois Lane." Sydney starts giggling, and through her giggles she asks

Jimmy, "do you have has any ideas what couple we could be?" Jimmy thinks for a minute, and says, "how about Barney and Wilma Flintstone. Whiz says, "Ya ba da ba do" to Jimmy, and pretty soon the whole group was repeating, "Ya ba da ba doo." Sydney tells Jimmy, "how exciting, the Flintstones have always been my favorite cartoon. Let's hope the costume shop has everything we need."

The kids wildly paw through the costume racks. The shop is well supplied, but they only have a short time to find their outfits before they have to meet Rick. Sydney and Jimmy get lucky right away and find the Flintstone costumes. When the two of them try on their costumes, the other kids start calling them Fred and Wilma. Jimmy replies in character as Fred, "meet the new and improved Flintstones."

Sierra and Whiz are starting to panic because Superman has been a popular request this year, and the only size they can find is small. Whiz laughs when he tries it on, "I know I'm not a big guy, but doesn't this costume seem a little tight." The kids look at him, and they are trying not to laugh, as Sierra answers, "Whiz you look real cute in your outfit, and I don't think it's too tight." Whiz mumbles, "okay if you are sure it looks okay." The other kids are still giggling, as Whiz walks back to the dressing room.

Sierra looks just like Lois Lane in her get-up. She tells the other kids, "I'm going to wear my hair in a matronly bun, and go to the dollar store for reading glasses that will complete my outfit."

Amie and Kevin try on Munster outfits. Kevin comes out of the dressing room walking like Herman, at the same time as Amie is prancing around with her long black wig on, and Kevin calls her Lillie dear. All the kids look at each other and Kevin says, "we are going to be a big hit at the dance." Amie blushes, as Kevin looks proudly at her, "you are the prettiest girl in school."

They pay for their purchases, and hurry back to meet Rick, who is pacing in front of McDonald's even though they return early. They say their good-byes to their friends, calling them by their costume names.

The four kids get back to the marina a little early, and wait with nervous anticipation. Amie is shaking on the inside, scared, and her stomach is in knots, but she forces a smile, so the boys won't notice her fear.

Hud arrives in his car, and a large van with ten seal members pull in behind him. Hud walks over to Rick's car, with a John Wayne swagger, and thanks the kids again for the excellent job of getting information about the yacht. As Hud is talking, Whiz is thinking that Hud is a very imposing looking guy, I don't think I would want to mess with him, even with my karate training. Hud asks Rick to point out the yacht that Stevens is on, and Rick shows him the yacht. Hud says to his men, "the yacht is within swimming distance, and that's good because we can sneak up on them."

Hud and his ten men suit up, with all of their waterproof equipment. Everything they have is black, and they look like shadowy figures in the night. It is dark now, as the men get in the water, and swim the approximate mile to the huge yacht The men have small microphones and earpieces so they can communicate with each other. When they get close enough to the yacht, Hud signals to the troop to shoot the ropes, and climb up the side of the ship.

The yacht is heavily guarded, but the Navy Seal members have done this type of mission several times, and know exactly what to do. When they reach the top, Hud gives the go ahead to rush the men who are on deck. The first six men are taken very easily with the seal member's expertise. A second group of men have been alerted, and come rushing out of the stairway with their guns blazing, and two of the Seal members are shot. Hud sees two of his men are injured, and he commands his men to take the remainder of the men down, at any cost

Hud quickly shoots out the lights of the ship. The Stevens men can't see the Seal men in the darkness, and they hesitate to shoot. This is when the Seal members move in and take over, with their night goggles on, they round up the Stevens men with little more than a scuffle.

Hud sees a man run, and jump off the side of the ship, into a speedboat. He knows he won't be able to catch him, so he quickly calls Rick on his cell phone, and says, "it is up to you to try and catch a man that is leaving the yacht. I think the man is Robert Stevens." Rick replies, "we'll do our best to catch him."

The kids can't see the speedboat coming in the dark, but they wait on the pier where they had seen Stevens leave from. The day had been so bright and sunny, but now with all of the clouds it is pitch black out. Whiz gets his helmet with the light on it out of the car, and all four kids get in position. Amie feels a loud pounding from under her blouse where her heart is, and thinks to herself, she will never get used to this kind of danger. Rick and Jimmy are both thinking they don't want to mess up, because of the faith, Hud has in them. In just a few minutes they can hear the roar of the powerful engine of the speedboat. Robert Stevens climbs out of the boat, and ties it to the dock, as all four kids jump him. It is so dark out the kids can't see where to punch the man. Stevens grabs Amie around the neck, and yells, "I have a gun pointed to the girl's head, and I will shoot if you don't back off." The kids have no choice but to do what he says. Stevens walks to his car with his arm around Amie's neck, "you are going with me." Amie looks up and can see the man's sneering face, and her stomach tightens even more.

Her hands begin to shake and are curled into fists. She is thinking, I know I can get away, this maneuver has been practiced a hundred times in karate school. Amie starts to cry, and the man loosens his chokehold just long enough for Amie to spin around, and kick the man in the groin. As the man hollers in pain Amie runs back to where the other kids are. Stevens limps as fast as he can to his car, and squeals past the kids. Rick and the other kids, hug Amie, as she is still crying. Rick gives her a special bear hug, "great job getting away, I knew that karate school would pay off."

Back on the yacht the Seal team is searching for the President with flashlights. Finally down in a dark dingy space, not big enough for a dog, they find the President all scrunched up. He is alive, but very cold and stiff as a board from the curled up position he has been in for so long. Hud calls Christine, as she has been waiting in a coast guard helicopter, his excitement peaks as he tells her, "the President is alive and well." Christine is overwhelmed with the news, and tells Hud in a joyful tone, "we will be landing on the yacht in just a few minutes." Hud informs the weary President, "a helicopter is on the way, and they will take you to Walter Reed." The President shakes Hud's hand, as he is helped to a nearby chair. Hud tells one of his men, "go to the galley and find some hot tea, to warm the President up." While they are waiting for help, Hud remains with the President, until Christine and the Coast Guard arrive, and take him to the hospital to be checked over.

Rick calls Hud, "Robert Stevens got away. He had a gun and got the drop on us. But the good news is, there is a GPS tracking device in his car, and we can track where he goes. He can run but he can't hide for long."

Hud tells one of his Seal team members, " call Naval Intelligence, and pick up the captured criminals from the ship, and throw their butts in the Navy Brig for now, and have the officer in charge start interrogating them."

Hud decides to ride to Walter Reed with the President, and Christine. The Coast Guard Captain gets the okay from the air tower for take off. He expertly guides the noisy helicopter safely off the ship, and into the dark of the night.

As they fly off, again the President says to Hud, "thank you for saving me, I appreciate you going the extra mile, and coming along with me for my flight to the hospital." Hud goes on to tell him, "I had a lot of help in locating you." The President asks, "who else was involved in my rescue?" Hud smiles, "you are going to find this hard to believe Mr. President, but the brains of your return happens to be four kids, in fact three of them are under sixteen years of age." The President asks in a stunned voice, "what kids, how could kids know where I was hidden out?" Hud answers, "it is a long story, and after I get some information from you, we'll get back on the subject of the kids." The President answers, "you know best, give me another cup of tea and let's get to it." Hud asks, "what do you know about the actual crash of the helicopter?" President McQueen replies, "that was all staged, everyone was taken off the helicopter before they blew it up, so no one was hurt." The President tells Hud, "I need to call my Press Secretary, and let him know that I am still alive, so he can make an announcement on TV to the country, that I am alive and well." Hud says, " I'm afraid you will have to appoint a new one. It was

Robert Stevens that was behind all of this." The President thoughtfully replies, "I have thought something fishy was going on in that office for the last few months."

Shortly they are at the hospital; and the weakened President is wheeled in with the awaiting servicemen escorting him into the emergency room. Hud and Christine are right beside the President until the team of doctors takes over. Hud salutes the President; "Christine and I have some unfinished business to take care of." The President says to Hud, "when the doctors are through with me we need to meet for another briefing about my kidnapping." Hud replies, "good idea, the staff here will take good care of you, and I'll see you soon."

Christine calls her men and asked, "have you picked up David Ferris? He's the man who is running against the President in the up and coming election." The FBI agent answers her, "we were lucky, he was home in bed sleeping like a baby that is until we interrupted him." "Congratulations," she says. The FBI agent tells her, "Ferris is singing like a bird about Stevens involvement in the President's kidnapping." Christine says, "wonderful, keep on questioning him to see if you can find out where Stevens might be headed."

It is late and Hud and Christine decide to get a little shut-eye and pick up in the morning to find Stevens.

The next morning all of the TV channels are announcing to the nation that the President has been found alive. The announcer states, "the President is fine both physically and mentally. In fact he is planning to be in his office in a few hours where he is expected to formally announce to America that he is still planning on running for re-election. He also is planning a press conference that has been arranged by his new Press Secretary Mr. Jacob Withers." Most of the reporters are speculating that maybe the former Press Secretary was involved with the kidnapping of the President.

Rick and the twins are intensely watching the news. After the special news announcement Rick is upset that Robert Stevens got away from them last night. Rick hits his fist on the table, and says to the twins "I blew it!" Amie says to Rick, "if you had a gun we would have been on equal terms with him, and we probably would have captured him." Rick says, "that's part of the reason I'm so upset, I have a license for a concealed weapon which I keep in the trunk. I should have had it available in case I needed it." Unknown to the kids Tom and Lois Winters are listening at the door as Lois gives a loud gasp discovering the danger her children placed themselves in.

The Winters parents walk in the room with their children, you could have heard a pin drop as the kids discovered their conversation had been overheard by their parents. The color was drained from their mom's face, and their dad starts speaking in a loud voice, almost shouting to them. "I demand to know everything you kids have been up to."

Rick says, "let me explain how we got caught up in this. First of all you need to know that I am a licensed Private Investigator," his dad interrupts and asks, "what happened to your law degree?" Rick answers his dad, trying to talk in a calm voice, "I had enough college credits in law school to become a P.I., the only thing that was lacking was to take the state exam, which I passed in flying colors." Mr. Winters says to him, "that's well and fine, but right now I want to hear about last night, and all of the other shenanigans you kids have been up to." Rick says to his dad, "okay I'll start from the beginning, but you had better sit down, it is a long story."

Jimmy gets in the conversation, talking in an excited voice, "it wasn't Rick's fault." Mr. Winters says to Jimmy, "go on young man and finish explaining."

Jimmy clears his throat as he is telling his parents, "remember when Johnny read the mind of Robert Stevens on TV." They both nod their heads, "keep talking" his mother says, as Jimmy goes on, "I know we are going to be grounded when I tell you what we did." Lois says to Jimmy, "quit stalling and tell us what's been going on." "When we went to the White House tour with our class last summer, Amie, Whiz and I planted surveillance bugs in Robert Stevens office." "You did what," Tom yells and asks Rick, "did you know about this?" Amie butts in and says, "Dad please listen, it's not Rick's fault. We decided to do it on our own, and you have to remember, because of the bugs the President was rescued." Mrs. Winters takes a deep breath and says, "that's true, the President is safe because of our kids, and that is a terrific feeling." Mr. Winters says, "I am proud of my children but they could have been killed. I don't like the idea of you kids risking your lives for anyone. You are just children and that's what I want you to be. Leave the crime solving to the adults who are trained for this. Now I want you to promise me, from here on in you are just going to be typical teenagers, and quit dragging poor Whiz in on all of this stuff too. He's just a kid and something worse then kidnapping could have happened to him, and then how would you feel?" Amie hugs her Dad, and tells him, "we are really sorry, we didn't think about the consequences if something went wrong. Jimmy and I promise we'll just be kids." Rick says, "Dad I will make sure this doesn't happen again." Mr. Winters replies, "you better young man. Amie and Jimmy, I will talk to you about your punishment after Mother and I decide together what your punishment should be. Now leave us alone to talk to Rick."

The twins leave the room, and both parents look at Rick as he starts telling them about becoming a Private Investigator. Mr. Winters asks, "what about your law degree?" "I'm still planning on getting my degree; I can finish my classes through the Internet." Mrs. Winters, with a worried look on her face tells Rick, "I know being a P.I. is a very honorable profession, but it is a lot more dangerous than becoming an attorney." "Mom I have a fifth sense that P.I.'s need to be good. I am a natural at it, and it is something that I want to do." Mr. Winters looks at his wife and says, "I guess the boy has made up his mind." Mrs. Winters gets up and hugs Rick; "whatever you decide I know you will be good at it." Tom also hugs Rick, "I have known some very successful P.I.'s, in fact I can make some good contacts for you." "Thank you both for understanding, and I will make you proud." Tom says, "we know you will son. Now what should we do about the twins?" Lois says to her husband, "why don't you give them a break, they promised you they will stay out of trouble, and because of their actions we still have our President." Good point Mr Winters says, "but we can't let them off scot-free." Mrs. Winters says, "you are right. I have an idea, why don't we have them do some community service work, like performing at the homeless shelter with Johnny and Barbie, to raise money for winter coats and blankets." "Wonderful idea he says now let's call them back to give them the news of their punishment."

Mr. Winters is looking sternly at his children as he informs them of their punishment. They are both overjoyed, Amie is yelling "whoopee" and Jimmy is dancing around the floor with relief. Jimmy tells Amie, "lets go upstairs and tell the parrots to start rehearsing, we have a gig to do."

The first order of business is for the twins to start acting like kids again. The Halloween dance is Friday night after the school football game. The twins are only thirteen years old, and are not allowed to have dates. Mrs. Winters has arranged with the other kids parents to have everyone meet at their house, and she has reassured the parents, "I have made arrangements for our kids to be chaperoned." What the twins didn't know as a surprise. Hud and Christine is going to drive them to the school and also are going to the dance with them as their chaperones.

At last Friday night is here, Amie and Jimmy gulped down their dinner so they can go upstairs to get ready for the night festivities. Amie is allowed to wear a lot of eye make-up for this special event. Mrs. Winters helps her to apply all of the eye goop. Amie says, "look how big my eyes look with all this make-up on. Can I start wearing eye make up everyday?" Mrs. Winters says, "sure when you are about thirty-five." Mrs. Winters helps her daughter fix her long black wig, now she looks just like Lillie Munster. Mrs. Winters stands back from Amie and says to her, "you are a beautiful girl even with all of that make up on."

When they walk downstairs everyone there is dressed in full costumes ready to go. The doorbell rings, Jimmy rushes to the door, and is surprised to see Hud and Christine standing there dressed as characters from the movie Grease. Christine is wearing her hair into a high ponytail, and has on a full skirt with a poodle sewn on it. Hud has his hair slicked back in a greasy looking duck tail, complete with black leather jacket and Levi's, with the cuffs rolled up. The kids are happy to see them, and Hud says, "let's get going we are taking all of you to the dance."

Mrs. Winters quickly grabs her camera and gets a picture of this unsightly group. Rick is standing on the stairs waving good bye to everyone. Amie says, "c'mon Rick hurry and get ready and go with us." He replies, "I had planned on riding with you guys but, I'm waiting for an attorney to call me back. She is looking for a private investigator to work with her in her new law office. I say office; it's just her and her secretary that works there. She's about my age and hasn't been in business very long." "What's her name," Mr. Winters asks? "Her name is Annette Duncan, a pretty little thing with the biggest bluest eyes I have ever seen." Tom and Lois look at each with a wondering look. "Anyway," Rick says, "as soon as she calls, I'll get ready and meet you guys at school."

Hud opens the front door and tells the kids, "see that limousine over there that's our ride." Sierra says, "wow what a ride". Whiz looks at her; "nothing's too good for Superman's girl Lois Lane." Kevin dressed in his Herman Munster attire says to Amie, "and nothing's too good for my Lillie." Jimmy who looks surprisingly like Barney turns to Sydney and repeats, "nothing is too good for my girl Wilma," and the whole crowd joins in chanting, "ya ba da ba doo."

Soon they are at the school and, Jimmy says, "I don't recognize anyone." Whiz who is starting to feel very uncomfortable in his tight Superman costume, says, "I hope they don't recognize me in this tight suit." The kids start laughing and Sierra tells him, "you will be recognized." Whiz mumbles, "that's what I was afraid of."

Sierra says, "forget about them and let's dance." "Good idea," as he grabs Sierra's hand and the two of them start dancing around the floor. Whiz with his cape flapping, up in the air, look's like he could take off and fly away.

The other couples join Whiz and Sierra on the dance floor. They motion for Hud and Christine to get out on the floor to dance. Hud shakes his head no, "have a good time kids, we are going to wait for a nice slow song."

Back at home, at last Rick receives his call from Annette Duncan. Rick is trying not to show his excitement of hearing her voice. Her voice is sounding very professional, as she tells him, "I have consulted with my secretary, and if you are still interested, the job is yours as the office P.I." "Great when do I start?" Annette replies, "how does Nine o'clock on Monday sound?" "Perfect I'll be there and thank you for the opportunity." Annette continues on, "what I really like about you is, you are young, just as I am and I think we both have a lot of fresh ideas." Rick says, "your right and because we are both young and not married (he thinks to himself clever, now I can find out if she is married) we can work long hard hours if we need to." She agrees, and adds, "both my secretary and myself like the idea that you are single for that very reason." Rick wonders if he noticed a little bit of excitement in her voice as she speaks. Annette tells him, "I am running late, I am supposed to go to the Halloween dance in Roseville tonight." Rick says, "you're kidding that's just where I'm going, I'm suppose to meet my brother and sister there." Annette tells him, "I'm going to meet my niece, she wants me take pictures of her and her friends. She also expects me to dress up so I have to hurry." Rick says, "I'll see you there, I'll be dressed as Sherlock Holmes," and what will you be dressed as? "I'll be the not so good-looking bag lady." Rick doesn't say this to her, but he is thinking she would look great in a burlap bag. He says, "I'll be looking for you." Rick can hardly wait to get to the dance to see Annette. He hurries and gets into his Sherlock Holmes costume.

Rick dresses quickly in his plaid suit with matching hat. He found an old spyglass in the attic, and looks for a mustache. At last he finds it and carefully places it above his upper lip. He takes a good look at himself in the mirror, and says out loud, "Sherlock my good man you're a fine looking chap."

As soon as Rick gets to the dance he looks for Hud and Christine. He sees them over by the punch bowl watching the twins. He approaches them and asks, "has anyone seen my man Watkins?" They look at Rick in his get-up and Hud asks, "is that you Rick?" He replies, "no I'm Sherlock Holmes." Christine and Hud laugh together and Christine says to Rick, "you make a fine Sherlock Holmes." Rick tells them, "I'm expecting to meet Annette Duncan here and I'm going to go look for her." Hud says, "before you leave to look for Annette, we need to talk to you about a few things." Rick replies, "how about we go for coffee after the dance and talk then." "It's a date we'll meet at Webber's Coffee Shop about midnight." "Great I'll see you guys later."

The dance is moving along nicely with all the kids in their many costumes dancing to the music. Suddenly the music stops and the Principal takes the mike to make an announcement. "We have a surprise event planned for tonight." The kids look on stage and there is Johnny and Barbie all dressed up as Batman and Robin. The kids start clapping as the birds sing the Monster Mash. The music is playing loudly and Johnny is hamming it up singing as loud as he can. The two parrots sing more Halloween songs, and then they sing some slow love songs that everybody dances to, including the parents. Rick has found Annette Duncan, and the two of them dance as close as they can to each other, and it looks like Rick has found his true love. Everybody at the dance is in a festive mood when the dance comes to a close.

Hud and Christine meet Rick and Annette at the gourmet coffee shop. Rick introduces his date, "meet my new boss," and Annette says, "more like partners." Rick and Annette both order Chai tea. Annette says, "boy this is a good sign, our first date and we both like the same thing," Rick smiles and says, "Ya that's great," he is a little flustered by this beautiful girl, that is dressed as a bag lady.

Hud and Christine are sitting close to each other; Hud has his arm around Christine, they both say in unison, "I had a great time at the dance."

The silence is broken when Rick asks Hud, "what have you found out about Robert Stevens, and what is going on with the men that kidnapped my mother?

Annette is looking on intently because she doesn't know anything about what has happened. Christine tells them, "Robert Stevens car was found at J.F.K. airport in New York, City, but there is no record of him taking a flight anywhere." Hud says, "he probably used a fake identification." Annette says very excitedly, "I'm sorry to butt in, but are you the people that were involved with the kids that helped rescue the President?" Rick looks admiringly at Annette; she was so quick to pick up on what Hud was talking about. Rick catches his breath and shakes his head yes. "Can you believe it was not only I, but also my thirteen-year-old twin siblings and their friend Whiz. That's not the only help we had, remember Johnny the Parrot who performed at the dance, the bird who was dressed like Batman, he also helped, but I'll tell you about him another time."

Hud interrupts, "okay you two let's get back to business. The men that kidnapped your Mother are now in jail spilling their guts out. They'll be going to trial soon. We believe that everyone that was involved has been caught except for Robert Stevens."

While Rick is at the coffee shop, the Winters family and the six kids that rode with them to the dance arrive home in the limousine. All of the kids are laughing and talking nosily all the way home. When they get home their friends call their parents to pick them up. While they are waiting for their parents Johnny and Barbie are in the living room singing and dancing for them. At last the parents pick up the twin's friends, and the party is over.

Amie and Jimmy start to go to their rooms to get ready for bed. Mrs. Winters tells them, "as soon as Rick gets home your father and I have some news to tell you." She no sooner got that out of her mouth than Rick walks in the front door. Jimmy tells Rick, "hurry and set down, mom and dad need to talk to us." Rick gets a worried look on his face; he is thinking oh no, they are going to go through with the divorce. Tom enters the room and sees the worried look on Rick's face. He starts the family meeting by saying; "you know how important the three of you are to both your mother and I." Lois is sitting there not with a concerned look, but she is beaming at Tom. Rick notices right away, and breathes a sigh of relief. "Dad, please hurry and tell us the news." Amie is starting to cry and says, "please dad, don't tell us you and mom are going to get a divorce." Dad hugs her and says, "quite the opposite young lady. We realized through our separation how important it is for your Mother and I to stay together. We love each other very much." Lois is crying tears of joy as she looks at Tom with deep love in her eyes. Lois says, "we are sorry we put you children through our separation, and we have learned that marriage and children come before anything else." The three children run to their Mom and Dad hugging and crying.

Saturday morning is here too soon, the twins are still sleeping, when they hear Rick in the hallway, yelling, "whoopee, whoopee" at the top of his lungs. "C 'mon you guys get up and come downstairs the President is on TV. He is giving a news interview with details of his rescue. He just now mentioned that if it had not been for the help of three young, teen-agers and an older brother, taking matters into their own hands, he might not have been discovered for a long time." Now he's talking about Hud's navy seal men making the actual rescue. They both run downstairs half asleep, Jimmy asks, "is this a dream or is this for real?" "Amie tells him, "we are awake, pay attention to the President talking." The President goes on to say, "of course there are a few more people involved with my rescue, but for security reasons they cannot be identified. You know who you are and I can't thank you enough. Before the elections occur, I would like to invite all of the people and their families who helped save me, to the White House for a special party. My secretary will be contacting all of you and I sure hope you can make it. Also, I am going to present special awards of bravery medals and plaques, to the young people and to the Navy Seal Members. Again I want to thank you from the bottom of my heart, you are my heroes."

Jimmy and Amie are beaming, as Johnny is squawking, "that was fun maybe he'll get kidnapped again." Jimmy says, "no Johnny we don't want that to ever happen again." Maybe somebody else will get kidnapped to give you something to do."

As soon as the interview ends, the Winters telephone is ringing. Amie rushes to answer the phone. Her eyes are dancing with excitement, as she puts her hand over the phone and yells, "it's the President's secretary, she wants to know if we can attend the party." Mrs. Winters takes the phone from Amie to confirm, "we will be honored to attend." The secretary tells Mrs. Winters, "call me back when you have a list of everybody that is going to attend." Mrs Winters asks, "how many can we bring?" The secretary replies, "as many as you want." Mrs. Winters says, "thank you very much," I'll call you back with the number of people that will be attending."

Lois asks Mrs. Bellinger, "join us for breakfast, we are going to have another family meeting over breakfast and we want you to be included. This time it will be a joyful meeting, for a change no one is in trouble, everyone pitch in and get the table set." The twins scurry to the kitchen and quickly set the table. Mrs. Bellinger and Lois put the pancakes and eggs on the table as Rick butters the toast. Even Tom pitches in and pours the orange juice and coffee. Rick pulls out the chairs for Mrs. Bellinger and Lois to set on. At last they all are seated for breakfast.

Jimmy looks at his mom, "please tell us when the party is." Mr. Winters says, "okay Mother, I think we have held the kids in enough suspense, please give all of us the details of the party." "The party is going to be on Monday night, that is only two days away. It is a short notice, but the President wants to honor all of you before he gets busy with the election." Amie asks, "this is incredibly awe-some, can we invite Sydney and

Kevin?" Mr. Winters answers, "yes" and he tells Rick, " bring along your girlfriend also."

Rick immediately calls Annette, and asks, "would you like to go to the White House gala with me?" Annette says shrieking, "you got to be kidding." Rick answers, "our whole family is going to go, along with Whiz, and his family." Annette says, "WOW meeting you has really been special." Rick adds, "it has been special for me too. Now say yes, you'll go with me." Okay, you twisted my arm I'll go.

Rick also calls Hud to see if he and Christine are going. Hud says, "we had better not, we would blow our cover." "I have an idea," Rick said, "why can't you go as our family members?" Hud answers, "that's a good idea, I'll call my superior and get permission. My men will not be able to go, as they will be on another mission." After the twins call Kevin and Sydney, the Winters family sits down to watch television. They are all so excited, everyone is talking at once about the party, unaware what program is on. Finally Mr. Winters takes the remote and shuts off the television.

Johnny and Barbie join the family asking, "are we going to the party too?" Rick tells Johnny, "I'm sorry buddy, we cannot risk having your mind reading talents exposed. You would be placed in immediate danger, and all the thugs in the world would want to kidnap you, and use you to help them in all kinds of criminal activities." Mr. Winters walks over to the birds; "it's our job to protect you." Johnny still not convinced squawks, "you know I can only read minds for a short time, and then I get a migraine headache." Tom looks at Johnny, "this is the first that I have heard of that. Regardless of how long you can read minds, it is still too dangerous for you, if the wrong people found out." Johnny and Barbie hang their heads low, the twins rush up to them, Jimmy rubs Johnny's head and says, "we'll make it up to you, you are the real hero."

Amie gives Barbie a hug, "wait a minute," she says, "I have a great idea, after the President's party, we'll come back here and have a private party, to honor Johnny." The birds pick up their heads. Johnny asks, "are we going to have ice cream too?" Amie replies, "we'll have anything you two want." Johnny says, "beer too," Mrs. Bellinger looks at the birds with love, "anything but beer, but we'll have a very special party." The parrots scamper upstairs with Johnny singing to Barbie, "You Are My Special Angel." "Quite a pair those two," Tom said, and Lois nods in agreement.

The rest of the evening Amie is talking to her Mother about what dress to wear. Lois brings down a lovely pink velvet dress for Amie to try on. "I was saving this dress to give to you for our holiday party. I think it would be very appropriate to wear to the Awards ceremony." Amie rushes over to her mom; "this dress is beautiful. Can I try it on?" "Of course you can dear," mom said. Amie says, "be back in a flash." After quite a few minutes pass, Amie sashays down the stairs, "do I look beautiful or what?" Lois looks at her daughter, "I knew when I saw that dress, it would look great on you. Turn around and let me get a good look." Rick, "whistles" as Amie twirls around. "Pink is your most becoming color, Tom says to his daughter." Amie says, "it fits perfectly, I love the bow on the front and the belt makes my waist look so small."

Mrs. Winters says to her sons, "I might as well give you your holiday clothes too. I hope you are as happy as Amie is with her new dress." Lois reaches behind the couch and hands Rick and Jimmy there new suits. "Try them on boys, in case Mrs. Bellinger needs to alter them." After the boys dress, they come downstairs and stand next to Amie. Tom and Lois look at their family beaming with pride even Mr. Winters looks a little teary-eyed. "Drat it" he says, "I have something in my eye."

Monday night is here already, and everybody is dressed and ready to go to the White House. Jimmy says to his mom, "thanks for not picking out pink ties to go with Amie's dress." I thought about it for a minute just to get a rise out of you, but luckily I didn't have that much time to shop."

The Winters family, get into their station wagon, and Rick gets in his Mustang. Rick is going to pick up Annette, Sydney, and Kevin, and will meet the family at the White House. Hud, and Christine will also meet them at the White House. They don't want to blow their undercover identities, and they will be introduced as Lois's brother and sister in law. The entire Alfred Barnett's (alias Whiz) family will be there too.

When they arrive, they have to go through the large White House security gates and metal detectors. When inside the large ballroom, where the event is taking place, they are greeted, but Tom Winters is the only one that knows anybody. Tom proudly escorts his family around the room introducing them to all of the important people that are here.

Jimmy spots Whiz and asked his parents, "can Amie and I be excused to meet up with the Whiz and Sierra? Tom looks at them, "okay, but please behave like ladies and gentlemen." "We will," Amie says, as Jimmy is waving to the Whiz to get his attention.

Whiz and Sierra are standing in the middle of some elderly looking guests. Whiz is starving, and when the waiter comes by with the canape tray and offers some to Whiz, he grabs a handful, of what he thinks are little party cakes. He stuffs them in his mouth, and all of a sudden is making the most ghastly sounds, shouting, "ugh what is this crap, I thought it was candy or cake."

Amie says to Whiz, "shh, people are staring at you." Whiz takes his cocktail napkin and spits his food into it. Amie is looking mortified as the dignified guests turn and stare at them. "Haven't you ever had Sushi before," Jimmy asked? "Not only have I never had it, I don't even know what it is." Jimmy says, "it's raw eel." Whiz immediately starts gagging, and puts his leftovers back on the waiter's tray. As all of this is going on the President is observing, the embarrassing predicament the children are in. He walks over to Whiz, "I never cared for Sushi either, waiter please go in the kitchen and find some hot dogs, or something these young people will enjoy. As a matter of fact a hot dog sounds good to me too."

The President seeks out Rick, and says to him, "before I make my speech on TV I would like a few details on how you kids discovered that Robert Stevens was a bad guy." Rick explains to the President all about the bathroom incident, how Jimmy overheard Robert Stevens, on his cell phone in the bathroom, when the twins and Whiz went on a school tour of the White House.

It is time for the President to speak on National Television, and he starts by telling the world, it seems, "I was saved because one of these kids got sick." He goes on to explain, "one of the kids, got sick during a White House tour, and needed to use a bathroom right away. The tour guide let him use the executive bathroom, and while he was in there, Robert Stevens entered his office, not knowing that anyone was in his bathroom. The young man overheard Stevens talking on his cell phone, to another bad guy, about getting rid of the President, before the up and coming election." The President asks the four young people, " come to the front and receive your medals." As they walk to the podium the crowds stands up applauding.

The President places the beautiful medals around each of the kids neck, and shakes their hands. When he presents the Whiz his medals he asks him, "did you enjoy your hot dog? Whiz who is not known for his shyness says, "yes sir it was the best hot dog I have ever had." The crowd again applauds the children. The President tells the crowd, "these young people are trying to make our country a better place. I think I can speak for all of us, the world is a better place because of them, and others like them."

The President asks Lois and Tom Winters, " please stand up, I want our guests to meet the parents of these brave young people." They both stand and Tom salutes the President. Lois has tears in her eyes, she blows a kiss to the kids and tells them she loves them. The audience again applauds. The President motions for the respectful crowd to quiet down as he has some other things to say. "Let me give you a little background about Tom and Lois. Tom has worked for the FBI for a number of years; this is where his children have inherited their bravery. Lois is a school teacher and this is where the children inherited their brains." The crowd laughs and the President says, "just kidding Tom." When Tom got wind of what his children were up to he immediately stepped in and contacted NCIS to take over the rescue of myself. Tom and Lois after finding out what their kids were up to, as to be expected were very concerned about their safety. They wanted to ground them for life that's how scared they were. At any rate you can see they were not grounded for life as they are all here. They have promised their parents from now on, they will leave the cloak and dagger to trained professionals. Thank you Mr. and Mrs. Winters for listening to your children." The crowd again applauds as they both sit down.

The President goes on to explain the involvement of the Navy Seals Members. "They are not here tonight because they have to remain under cover for their future missions. I also want to thank a couple of other people who shall remain nameless for the same reasons. If it were not for all of you I might be dead or worse yet, the United States of America might have a new President who is very corrupt. We all thank you for putting a stop to his plan." The audience applauds again.

The children are still standing on stage; Jimmy is applauding loudly and whistling at the same time. Amie tries to get Jimmy to quick whistling, but he pays no attention to her. Whiz takes his lead, and also starts whistling. The crowd laughs at them and the President steps in, and says, "it warms my heart to see you guys acting like typical teenagers." Amie standing there in her lovely pink dress looking like a beautiful young lady. Unlike the boys who are feeling a bit boisterous, she is feeling very emotional, and is trying to hold back tears as the President walks over and hugs her. He takes her hand and escorts her back to her seat. The boys walk off the stage as the crowd stands and applauds again, with some of the men in the audience whistling, just as the boys did on stage. Jimmy and Whiz gives them a thumbs up as they sit down.

There is about one hundred people in the ball room, and everybody gets in line to shake the Presidents hand, before they all sit down to a magnificent looking meal prepared by the White House staff. After the wonderful meal, and lots of conversation the President excuses himself saying, "I have to get up early tomorrow to start campaigning." On the way out he thanks everybody again.

Mrs. Bellinger and the parrots are home watching the festivities on television. When the boys whistle, the parrots start whistling. Mrs. Bellinger tells them, "whistle quietly, you are piercing my ears." Johnny asks her, "how do you whistle quietly?" To his surprise, this dignified elderly woman, puts her two fingers in her mouth, and gives off the loudest whistle the parrots have ever heard. "Okay, okay I get your point no more whistling."

After the program is over, Mrs. Bellinger prepares coffee, and hot chocolate, for when the family returns. She is still in the kitchen when she hears the twins, noisily open the door calling her name. "I'm in the kitchen," and the whole family gathers around the kitchen table showing her their medals. She admires them, and hugs the entire family. "Did you watch us on TV," Amie asks? "I sure did, the birds and I, enjoyed every second of it." Johnny looks admiringly at their medals. "Don't worry Mrs. Bellinger has made you one too," Amie says. Tom tells Jimmy, "run upstairs and get Johnny's medal; and we'll have our special ceremony for him now." Johnny asks, "will the President present it to me?" Rick says no, "remember we decided for your safety that no one could know about your involvement in saving the President. We do have someone special to give it to you," and in walks Hud and Christine. Jimmy hands the medal to

Hud as Johnny flies over to Hud, who then puts the medal around his neck. "I have always known what a special friend you are to me. Your talent for helping people in need is even hard for me to fathom. I think I speak for all of us, without you watching Stevenson on TV, picking up that he was out to get the President, none of us would have been able to find him so soon. Thank you buddy from all of us."

THE END